复旦大学外文学院 资助

归巢与启程
中澳当代诗选（中国卷，汉英对照）

Homings and Departures:
Selected Poems from Contemporary China and Australia
(China Volume, Chinese-English Version)

包慧怡 海岸 主编
Edited by Bao Huiyi & Hai An

青海人民出版社

图书在版编目（CIP）数据

归巢与启程：中澳当代诗选．中国卷：汉英对照 /
包慧怡，海岸主编．-- 西宁：青海人民出版社，2018.9
ISBN 978-7-225-05644-9

Ⅰ.①归… Ⅱ.①包…②海… Ⅲ.①诗集－中国－
当代－汉、英 Ⅳ.①I12

中国版本图书馆 CIP 数据核字 (2018) 第 213924 号

归巢与启程：中澳当代诗选（中国卷，汉英对照）
包慧怡　海岸　主编

出 版 人	樊原成
出版发行	青海人民出版社有限责任公司
	西宁市五四西路 71 号　邮政编码：810023　电话：（0971）6143426（总编室）
发行热线	（0971）6143516 / 6137730
网　　址	http://www.qhrmcbs.com
印　　刷	青海西宁印刷厂
经　　销	新华书店
开　　本	880mm × 1240 mm　1/24
印　　张	9.75
字　　数	70 千
版　　次	2018 年 10 月第 1 版　2018 年 10 月第 1 次印刷
书　　号	ISBN 978-7-225-05644-9
定　　价	30.00 元

版权所有　　侵权必究

前 言

两卷本双语诗集《归巢与启程——中澳当代诗选（中国卷）》是一份集体劳作的成果，是年轻的中澳创意写作中心(China-Australia Writing Centre) 献给广大诗歌爱好者的一份薄礼。2015年，中澳创意写作中心(CAWC) 由位于上海的复旦大学与位于澳大利亚的科廷大学共同成立，旨在推动中澳双方在创意写作领域的研究和实践，并为更多国际学者和作家搭建创作交流的平台。中心试图对传统的创意概念和界限进行突破，除文学创作外，它还涉及各类非文学的叙事创作，如新闻、历史等；复旦方面参与中心的主要院系是外文学院、中文系、历史系、新闻学院。三年来，在以复旦大学中澳创意写作中心主任院谈峥教授和科廷大学中澳创意写作中心前主任丽兹·布尔斯基副教授和现主任露西·杜根博士为首的多位老师的不懈推动下，CAWC 已在西澳弗里曼特尔市和中国上海市两地举办了三届国际创意写作研讨会，和多场小说、诗歌、非虚构写作领域的专题对话，来自中国、澳大利亚和世界各地的作家与学者围绕"变革时代的文学"、"全球化时代的文化认同"、"前瞻与回顾"

等主题展开了诸多有益的交流，这些交流的成果至今仍反哺着与会者的创作与研究。

"归巢与启程"是科廷大学CAWC、复旦大学CAWC以及堪培拉大学国际诗学研究中心(IPSI)诗歌合作出版长期项目的总称，主要由科廷大学CAWC主任露西·杜根博士，哇复旦大学CAWC副主任包慧怡博士，诗人、翻译家海岸，IPSI主任保罗·赫瑟里顿教授负责。除了《归巢与启程——中澳当代诗选》之《中国卷》与《澳洲卷》两本双语诗集外，该项目还计划陆续推出《探声：21世纪中澳诗歌评论集》等一系列双语诗论和诗歌翻译研究文集。

《归巢与启程——中澳当代诗选(中国卷)》选编了中国大陆26位在20世纪50—60年代出生，至今仍在坚持汉语写作的先锋诗人的作品，也收录了25位代表更年轻一代审美取向与文化观念的"70—90后"的诗人作品。本书以汉英双语形式呈现新世纪全球经济一体化背景下，具有悠久诗歌传统的中国当代诗歌的掠影。本书的诗歌英译大致可分为两类：学术翻译和诗人翻译。其中约二分之一的英译出自优秀的诗人、翻译家之手，如凌静怡、戴维·佩里、梅丹理、顾爱玲、乔直、夏柯智、奚密、西敏、温侯廷等，余下部分则由诗人、翻译家海岸、包慧怡等提供英译初稿，再分别与澳洲诗人卡桑德拉·阿瑟顿、卡拉瑟斯及美莲等合作完成。

本书的出版得到了复旦大学外文学院出版基金的资助，外文学院院长曲卫国教授、中澳创意写作中心现主任姜林静副教授、青海人民出版社总编辑马非老师等均为本书的问世做了诸多努力，谨在此一并致谢。因篇幅所限，本书目前只编入了以中文创作的中国籍诗人的作品，未来我们希望有机会将更广义上的当代华语诗歌写作成果呈现给读者。《归巢与启程——中澳当代诗选(澳洲卷)》正由我们在科廷大学的同仁们紧张编辑中,不久也将与读者见面。

从太平洋到印度洋,从北半球到南半球,连接我们的是语言和诗,还有字词之外的种种微光与深影。《归巢与启程——中澳当代诗选(中国卷)》是一本力图消弭地理和文化界限的选集,同时试图在差异中呈现高度个人化的心灵地貌。它记录着诗人、译者、编者们的"归巢和启程",也希望爱诗的读者可以在其中找到属于自己的家园或航向。

包慧怡

2018 年 8 月于上海

Foreword

Homings and Departures: Selected Poems from Contemporary China and Australia (2 vols) is the fruit of collaborative labour, a bilingual anthology edited by the China-Australia Writing Centre (CAWC), an international centre led by Curtin University in Perth (West Australia) and Fudan University in Shanghai (China). Since its establishment in 2015, CAWC has endeavoured to promote practice and research in multilingual creative writing and translation, and to create a communication platform for writers and scholars from China, Australia and all around the world. CAWC aims to redraw the traditional boundaries of creative writing, and engages in various non-fictional writing activities in fields such as journalism and history, besides creative writing per se. On the side of Fudan University, the main participating institutions include the College of Foreign Languages & Literature, Department of Chinese, Department of History and College of Journalism.

During the past three years, led by Prof Tan Zheng (former director of CAWC Fudan), Ass. Prof Liz Byrski (former director of CAWC Curtin) and Dr Lucy Dougan (current director of CAWC Curtin), the centre has successfully held three international symposiums and multiple Creative Conversations with featured themes in Fremantle, WA and Shanghai. Writers and scholars from all over the world had many fruitful conversations on themes like "Literature in the Age of Revolutions", "Self-Conception in the Age of Displacement, Diaspora, and International Travel" and "Looking Back, Looking Forward", the results of which continue to nourish their writing and research.

"Homings and Departures" is an ongoing joint poetry project between CAWC Curtin University, CAWC Fudan University, and the International Poetry Studies Institute (IPSI), University of Canberra. Mainly led by Dr Lucy Dougan at CAWC Curtin, Dr Bao Huiyi, vice-director of CAWC Fudan, Ass. Prof Li Dingjun (Hai An) at CAWC Fudan, and Prof Paul Hetherington, director of IPSI, this ongoing long-term project aims to continue publishing bilingual anthologies of Australian and Chinese poetry, as well as associated volumes of essays and critical works in the future.

The current anthology *Homings and Departures: Selected Poems from Contemporary China and Australia (China Volume)* collects works by 51 poets from mainland China, a growing group of cutting-edge pioneer poets publishing internationally in Chinese, among whom 26 were born before the year 1970, and 25 after. The book offers an introduction to Chinese poetry today in the shadow of a long poetic tradition and in the context of global culture in the twenty-first century. The Chinese texts are presented in the original as well as in English translation, half of which proceed from the hands of celebrated English-speaking scholars, poets and translators including: Andrea Lingenfelter, David Perry, Denis Mair,

Eleanor Goodman, George O'Connell, Lucas Klein, Michelle Yeh, Simon Patton and Austin Woerner. The remaining half are chiefly prepared by bilingual poets Hai An and Bao Huiyi, in cooperation with Australian poets Cassandra Atherton, a.j.carruthers and Amelia Dale.

Publication of the current volume is funded by the College of Foreign Languages & Literature, Fudan University. We particularly wish to thank, among others, Prof Qu Weiguo, dean of the College, Ass. Prof Jiang Linjing, current director of CAWC Fudan, and Ma Fei, Editor-in-chief of Qinghai People's Publishing House, whose support is indispensable to the coming out of this book. Our colleagues at CAWC Curtin are working on the editing of the Australia Volume of this bilingual anthology, which will meet its global readers in the near future.

From the Pacific to the Indian Ocean, from the northern hemisphere to the southern one, language and poetry, together with invisible lustres and shadows between the lines, keep linking us ubiquitously. *Homings and Departures: Selected Poems from Contemporary China and Australia* is an anthology that hopefully dissolves some geographical, linguistic and cultural watersheds, but also highlights the distinct spiritual topography of each individual poet. It has recorded the homecomings and departures of poets, translators and editors, and wishes to, with blessings from Euterpe, involve its readers in their own odyssey searching for homes, or for stranger voyages.

Bao Huiyi

Shanghai, August 2018

目 录 Contents

芒克　Mang Ke　　　　　　　　　　　　　1
　雪地上的夜　Night on the Snow-covered Ground
　阳光中的向日葵　Sunflower in the Sun

西川　Xi Chuan　　　　　　　　　　　　5
　起风　The Rise of Wind
　伴侣　Companion

臧棣　Zang Di　　　　　　　　　　　　　9
　我喜爱蓝波的几个理由　A Few Reasons I Like Rimbaud
　绝对审美协会　Association for Aesthetics without Compromise

王家新　Wang Jiaxin　　　　　　　　　13
　田园诗　Pastoral
　桔子　Tangerines

吉狄马加　Jidi Majia　　　　　　　　　17
　自由　Freedom
　时间　Time

高兴　Gao Xing　　　　　　　　　　　　22
　水鸟　Water Bird
　母亲　Mother

汪剑钊　Wang Jianzhao　　　　　　　　26
　比永远多一秒　A Second More Than Forever
　初春是冬天的一个伤口　An Early Spring is a Wound in
　　　　　　　　　　　　Winter

树才　Shu Cai　　　　　　　　　　　　　30
　莲花　Lotus
　安宁　Tranquility

车前子　Che Qianzi　　　　　　　　　　34
　无诗歌（选章）　No Poetry（excerpts）
　宇宙　Cosmos

李少君　Li Shaojun　　　　　　　　　　37
　四合院　The *Sihe* Courtyard
　流水　Running Water

目 录 Contents

周瓒　Zhou Zan　40
翼　Wings
致一位诗人，我的同行　For a Poet, My Confrere

周瑟瑟　Zhou Sese　43
人群中总有一个好看的　There Will Always Be a Nice-looking Girl in the Crowd
另一种爱　Another Kind of Love

翟永明　Zhai Yongming　47
渴望　Desire
独白　Monologue

张烨　Zhang Ye　51
忘川　The River Lethe
骷髅舞　Skeleton Dance

王寅　Wang Yin　57
白色的海洋　White Sea

晚年来得太晚了　The Evening of My Life Has Come Too Late

陈东东　Chen Dongdong　61
莫名镇　Unnamed Town
它仍是一个奇异的词　It's Still a Strange Word

海岸　Hai An　65
灯塔　Lighthouse
茶树　Tea Bushes

梁晓明　Liang Xiaoming　69
玻璃　Glass
各人　Each to Each

余刚　Yu Gang　73
故人的问候　Greetings from an Old Friend
温柔　Gentleness

王自亮　Wang Ziliang　78
握手　Hand-shaking

目　录 Contents

钟表店　The Clock Shop

陈先发　Chen Xianfa　　82
孤岛的蔚蓝　Lonely Island Sapphire
秋兴九章之五　Nine Poems on Inspirations of Autumn (5)

雷武铃　Lei Wuling　　86
冬天的树　Trees in Winter
白云（二）　White Clouds（Ⅱ）

海男　Hai Nan　　93
简约　Simplicity
西南之隅，无限美好　The Southwest Corner is of Infinite Beauty

潘洗尘　Pan Xichen　　97
残忍的秋天　The Cruel Autumn
盐碱地　Saline-Alkali Land

伊沙　Yi Sha　　100
车过黄河　Crossing the Yellow River
结结巴巴　Stutter

马非　Ma Fei　　104
一把铁锹　Shovel
伟大的战争　Great War

王敖　Wang Ao　　107
冬夜站在加油站我怕什么　Standing at the Gas Station on a Winter's Night, What am I Afraid of
新年夜话　New Year's Eve Talk

胡续东　Hu Xudong　　114
一个拣鲨鱼牙齿的男人　A Man Who Collects Sharks' Teeth
白猫脱脱迷失　The White Cat Toqtamish

冷霜　Leng Shuang　　118
我们年龄的雾　The Fog of Our Age
小夜曲　Serenade

目 录 Contents

黄茜　Huang Qian　　123
七年　Seven Years
死亡路过二十六年　The Dead Pass Through Twenty-Six Years

王璞　Wang Pu　　127
宝塔　The Reliquary
有关声音　On Sound

赵四　Zhao Si　　131
孩子　Children
叹息　Sighs

戴潍娜　Dai Weina　　134
塑料做的大海　Plastic Sea
仰光的情人　Rangoon Lover

康苏埃拉　Consuela　　138
尽管火种并不忠诚　Though The Fire's Faith Is Yet Wavering

缺席即永在　The Absent And The Everlasting

张定浩　Zhang Dinghao　　142
1825年12月14日　Dec. 14, 1825
纸箱子　Cardboard Boxes

肖水　Xiao Shui　　147
我们的粮食不多了　Our Grain is Running Out
渤海故事集（选二）　Gulf of Bohai（excepts）

胡桑　Hu Sang　　152
赋形者　The Shaper
任性的人　The Capricious

了小朱　Le Xiaozhu　　155
小淹留　Stranded a Little Longer
经验之谈　Voice of Experience

丝绒陨　Si Rongyun　　161
灰尘　Dust

目 录 Contents

童年玩伴　Childhood Playmates

包慧怡　Bao Huiyi　　166
岛屿生活　The Archipelago
关于抑郁症的治疗　On Curing Depression

秦三澍　Qin Sanshu　　170
低空　Low Altitude
醒世篇　Waking the World Chapter

甜河　Tian He　　175
雨地　In the Rain
真实　Real

蔌弦　Su Xian　　179
宿舍　Dormitory
为背景乐中的修草工而作　The Gardener in the Soundtrack

泉子　Quan Zi　　183
我宁愿看到的是一堆灰烬　I'd Rather See a Pile of Ashes

所以我爱你　So I Love You

贾勤　Jia Qin　　186
飞　Fly
爱　Love

茱萸　Zhu Yu　　190
梨花或者绝句　Pear Blossoms or Quatrains
沈复：浮槎遗事　Shen Fu: Old Stories of a Raft Which Drifts

张尔　Zhang Er　　194
布吉河小夜曲　Buji River Serenade
交通协奏曲　Traffic Concerto

黄礼孩　Huang Lihai　　197
我爱它的沉默无名　I Love Its Silence And Obscurity
伤口也在散发出光芒　The Wound Is Sending Forth Glory

冯娜　Feng Na　　200
出生地　Birthplace

目 录 Contents

回声 Echo

柏桦 Bai Hua　　　　　　　　　205
望气的人   The Air Alchemist
一切黑   Dark Matter

樊星 Fan Xing　　　　　　　　　208
北京 夏 二〇〇八   Beijing Summer 2008
广州假期   Canton Holiday

译者简介 TRANSLATORS BIOS　　213

芒克　Mang Ke

芒克（1950–），诗人，北京人。1978年与北岛创办《今天》，出版的诗集有《心事》《阳光中的向日葵》《芒克诗选》等。
Mang Ke (1950–), Chinese poet, born in Beijing. co-founded the poetry magazine *Today* with Bei Dao in 1978 and published books of poetry including *Matters of the Heart, Sunflower in the Sun, Selected Poems by Mang Ke.*

雪地上的夜

Night on the Snow-covered Ground

雪地上的夜

是一只长着黑白毛色的狗

月亮是它时而伸出的舌头

星星是它时而露出的牙齿

就是这只狗

这只被冬天放出来的狗

这只警惕地围着我们房屋转悠的狗

正用北风的

on the snow-covered ground night

is a dog with black and white fur

the moon is the tongue it sticks out

the stars are the teeth it bares

it's this dog

this dog set loose by winter

this dog vigilantly pacing around our home

那常常使人从安睡中惊醒的声音

冲着我们嚎叫

这使我不得不推开门

愤怒地朝它走去

这使我不得不对着黑夜怒斥

你快点儿从这里滚开吧

可是黑夜并没有因此而离去

这只雪地上的狗

照样在外面转悠

当然，它的叫声也一直持续了很久

直到我由于疲惫不知不觉地睡去

并梦见眼前已是春暖花开的时候

shouting at us

with the northern wind

that jolts us from our peaceful sleep

leaving me no choice but to push past the dog

and rush up to it in anger

leaving me no choice but to denounce the night

you better get out of here in a hurry

but the night never goes away

on the snow-covered ground the dog

is still out there pacing

and of course its shouts keep on

beyond falling asleep, exhausted

to dream of spring flowers blooming before my eyes

(tr. by Lucas Klein)

阳光中的向日葵 / Sunflower in the Sun

你看到了吗

你看到阳光中的那棵向日葵了吗

你看它，它没有低下头

而是把头转向身后

就好像是为了一口咬断

那套在它脖子上的

那牵在太阳手中的绳索

你看到它了吗

你看到那棵昂着头

怒视着太阳的向日葵了吗

它的头几乎已把太阳遮住

它的头即使是在没有太阳的时候

也依然在闪耀着光芒

你看到那棵向日葵了吗

Have you seen it ?

Have you seen that sunflower in the sunlight ?

Look- she never lowers her head

but turns herself away

as if to chew away

that rope around her neck

that drags her in the hands of the sun.

Have you seen it ?

Have you seen her lifting her head-

that sunflower glaring at the sun ?

Her head almost obscures the sun

Her head is still ablaze with light

even in the absence of the sun

Have you seen that sunflower ?

归巢与启程 Homings and Departures—— 中澳当代诗选（中国卷） Selected Poems from Contemporary China and Australia

你应该走近它

你走近它便会发现

它脚下的那片泥土

每抓起一把

都一定会攥出血来

You should approach it

When you come closer you will discover

underneath that patch of mudded soil

whenever you grasp a fistful

will always be gripped with blood

(tr. by Hai An & Sawako Nakayasu)

西川　Xi Chuan

西川（1963- ），诗人，翻译家，江苏徐州人。现为北京师范大学特聘教授，著有诗集《西川的诗》《小主意：西川诗选》《蚊子志》等。

Xi Chuan, Chinese poet and translator, born in 1963 at Xuzhou, Jiangsu Province, currently appointed as Distinguished Professor by Beijing Normal University, is author of several poetry books including *Poetry of Xi Chuan*, *A Small Idea: Selected Poems of Xi Chuan*, *Notes on the Mosquito*.

起风 / The Rise of Wind

起风以前树林一片寂静

起风以前阳光和云影

容易被忽略仿佛它们没有

存在的必要

起风以前穿过树林的人

是没有记忆的人

一个遁世者

起风以前说不准

是冬天的风刮得更凶

Before the rise of wind the woods were still

before the rise of wind sunlight and cloudiness

could be ignored for having

no *raison d'être*

before the rise of wind a man walking through the woods

was a man without memory

a recluse

before the rise of wind it couldn't be said

还是夏天的风刮得更凶

我有三年未到过那片树林

我走到那里在起风以后

whether winter wind

or summer wind was harsher

I haven't been to the woods in three years

I went there after the rise of wind

伴侣

我还不知道她是谁。

我还不知道她步入我的庭院推开我的房门是要找我还是要找另一个人。

她爬上我的床,睡在我的不眠之夜,有如一截白蜡丢失了她的火焰。

我抱起她来感觉翻越了一架高山。

半个月亮透过方形窗口照在我的前额,仿佛照在一个鬼影朦胧的方形广场,

至少那一夜我不曾侃侃而谈,

我不想惹她讨厌。

至少那一夜我几乎不曾呼吸,

因为她深沉的呼吸表明她孤单又疲倦。

哦,不,没有这样一个"她"用深沉的呼吸表明她孤单又疲倦。

没有哪一夜我几乎不曾呼吸否则我活不到今天。

我从不惹人讨厌。

Companion

I still don't know who she was.

I still don't know if she walked into my yard and opened my front door in search of me or someone else.

She climbed into my bed and slept through my insomnia like a white candle that had lost its flame.

Holding her I felt like crossing a mountain.

The half-moon shone onto my forehead through the rectangular window as if shining onto a public square through a ghostlike haze,

and at least that night I never spoke freely,

I didn't want to make her angry.

At least that night I barely breathed,

because her heavy breathing made clear she was lonely and weary.

我从不侃侃而谈那不是我的习惯。

我确曾漫步在方形广场，但从未发现那里鬼影朦胧。

我只允许圆满的月亮透过圆形窗口将我的前额照亮。

我从未翻越过高山，即使在想象中。

我从不失眠，即使有白蜡把蜡油滴在我的眼睑。

所以我不知道"她"是谁，这是当然。

Oh, no, there is to "her" whose loneliness or weariness could be made clear by heavy breathing.

No night during which I barely breathed, or I wouldn't be alive today.

I never make anyone angry.

I never speak freely it's not my style.

I have in fact strolled through the public square, but never felt any ghostlike haze.

I only allow the full moon to shine onto my forehead through round windows

I've never crossed mountains, haven't even imagine it.

And I never have insomnia, not even if hot wax were dripping from a white candle onto my eyelids.

So I don't know who "she" is, that much is certain.

(tr. by Lucas Klein)

臧棣　Zang Di

臧棣（1964-），诗人，北京人。北京大学中文系教授，出版有诗集《燕园纪事》《风吹草动》《新鲜的荆棘》《沸腾协会》和《慧根》等。

Zang Di, Chinese poet, born in 1964 in Beijing, currently the Professor of Chinese Language and Literature at Beijing University, is the author of several poetry books including *Memory of Yan Yuan*, *Wind Blows and Grass Wave* and *Fresh Thorns*, *The Seething Association* and *The Roots of Wisdom*.

我喜爱蓝波的几个理由

他的名字里有蓝色的波浪，
奇异的爱恨交加，
但不伤人。浪漫起伏着，
噢，犹如一种光学现象。
至少，我喜欢这样的特例——
喜欢他们这样把他介绍过来。
他命定要出生在法国南部，
然后去巴黎，去布鲁塞尔，
去伦敦，去荒凉的非洲
寻找足够的沙子。

A Few Reasons I Like Rimbaud

Lan-bo···in his name there are blue waves,
Strange combination of love and hate,
But not hurtful, in romantic undulations,
Ahh, like an optical phenomenon.
At any rate, I like a name to make sense for once—
I like the way they introduced him to us.
His fate was to be born in southern France,
Then go to Paris, then to Brussels,
Then to London, then to desolate Africa
To seek a sufficiency of sand.

他们用水洗东西，而他

用成吨的沙子洗东西。

我理解这些，并喜爱

其中闪光的部分。

我不能确定，如果早生

一百年，我是否会认他作

诗歌上的兄弟。但我知道

我喜欢他，因为他说

每个人都是艺术家。

他使用的逻辑非常简单：

由于他是天才，他也在每个人身上

看到了天才。要么是潜在的，

要么是无名的。他的呼吁

简洁但是复杂："什么?永恒。"

有趣的是，晚上睡觉时，

我偶尔会觉得他是在胡扯。

而早上醒来，沐浴在

晨光的清新中，我又意识到

他的确有先见之明。

They use water to wash things, but he

Used tons of sand to wash things.

I understand such doings and I find delight

In the part that sparkles.

I cannot be sure, had I been born

A century ago, if I would have treated him

As my brother in poetry. But I know

That I like him, because he said

Everyone is an artist.

The logic of his statement was simple:

Being a genius, he could see genius

In anyone. Perhaps it was latent,

Or maybe just nameless. His rallying cry

Was forthright yet complex: "What？Eternity."

Oddly enough, getting ready for bed at night,

I sometimes feel he was spouting nonsense,

But waking at morning, bathing in

The new day's pristine light, I realize

He had the gift of prophecy.

绝对审美协会

我蹲下来,我在等
细得像鞋带的蚯蚓说话。

我的四周是没膝高的油菜地,
自行车放倒一边,我像是已无路可迷。

成年后,每个人都声言
他们没见过会说话的蚯蚓。

这世界已足够小了,但我们还是
找不到你真正想要的东西。

蚯蚓先生,你知道你最渴望得到的
是什么吗?你身上的线

看上去太短小,就像是主动邀请我们

Association for Aesthetics without Compromise

I kneel down, waiting to hear

An earthworm thin as a shoelace speak.

Rapeseed grows up to my knees, my bike lays nearby.

It seems there's no more road to get lost from.

After coming of age, every person will tell you

They have never seen a talking earthworm.

This world is small enough already, but still

We haven't found what you are really after.

Mr. Earthworm, do you know what

You are really longing for ? The single stroke of your

 body

把你当成一个诱饵。

而你的身材细长，很适合在地下跳探戈。
这也是我尊敬你的地方。

我为你准备的耐心甚至超过了
我为我的生活准备的耐心。

我不介意你的性别，假如我邀请你做我的诗神，
你会在意这首诗里干净得没有一点土吗？

Looks so terribly small, as if you wish to invite us
To make bait of you.

Your long and thin body is suited to dancing a tango
  underground.
This is one more reason to respect you.

The patience I lavish on you even surpasses
The patience I put into daily life.

I don't care what sex you are, if I ask you to be my
  muse,
Will you mind a poem so clean that no dirt clings？

(2005) (tr. by Denis Mair)

王家新　Wang Jiaxin

王家新 (1957–)，诗人，翻译家，生于湖北丹江口。中国人民大学文学院教授，出版有诗集《纪念》《游动悬崖》《王家新的诗》《变暗的镜子》等。

Wang Jiaxin, Chinese poet and translator, born in 1957 at Danjiangkou. Hubei Province, currently the Professor of Chinese Literature at Renmin University of China at Beijing, is the author of several poetry books including *Commemoration, Moving Cliff, Poems of Wang Jiaxin, Darkening Mirror*.

田园诗

如果你在京郊的乡村路上漫游

你会经常遇见羊群

它们在田野中散开，像不化的雪

像膨胀的绽开的花朵

或是缩成一团穿过公路，被吆喝着

滚下尘土飞扬的沟渠

我从来没有注意过它们

直到有一次我开车开到一辆卡车的后面

Pastoral

On the country roads outside Beijing

you're sure to spot sheep

scattered over fields, like unmelted snow

or swollen blooms burst open.

they cross the road in clumps,

the herdsman barking them down

a weedy ditch, tripping and tumbling

through the dust.

在一个飘雪的下午

这一次我看清了它们的眼睛

（而它们也在上面看着我）

那样温良，那样安静

像是全然不知它们将被带到什么地方

对于我的到来甚至怀有

几分孩子似的好奇

我放慢了车速

我看着它们

消失在愈来愈大的雪花中

(2004)

I never paid much attention

until one afternoon

in flurries of snow

I nosed close behind a sheep truck,

the dark eyes gazing down

gentle and quiet, not knowing

where they were headed.

They turned toward me then,

curious as children.

I let the car drift back

through the thickening curtain of snow

and watched them disappear.

(2004)

桔子

整个冬天他都在吃着桔子，
有时是在餐桌上吃，有时是在公共汽车上吃，
有时吃着吃着
雪就从书橱的内部下下来了；
有时他不吃，只是慢慢地剥着，
仿佛有什么在那里面居住。

整个冬天他就这样吃着桔子，
吃着吃着他就想起了在一部什么小说中
女主人公也曾端上来一盘桔子，
其中一个一直滚落到故事的结尾……
但他已记不清那是谁写的。
他只是默默地吃着桔子。
他窗台上的桔子皮愈积愈厚。

他终于想起了小时候的医院床头

Tangerines

All winter he eats tangerines,
sometimes at the table,
　　sometimes on a bus.
Sometimes, as he's eating,
snow falls inside the bookcase.
Sometimes instead of eating,
　　he simply peels, slowly,
as if something lives within.

So he eats tangerines, all winter long,
and while eating recalls a novel
in which the heroine also brought to the table
a dish of tangerines. One kept rolling
　　till the end of the story.
But he can't name the author.
He simply eats the tangerine in silence.
The peels on his windowsill rise higher.

摆放着的那几个桔子，

那是母亲不知从什么地方给他弄来的；

弟弟嚷嚷着要吃，妈妈不让，

是他分给了弟弟；

但最后一个他和弟弟都舍不得吃，

一直摆放在床头柜上。

（那最后一个桔子，后来又怎样了呢？）

整个冬天他就这样吃着桔子，

尤其是在下雪天，或灰蒙蒙的天气里；

他吃得特别慢，仿佛

他有的是时间，

仿佛，他在吞食着黑暗；

他就这样吃着、剥着桔子，抬起头来，

窗口闪耀雪的光芒。

(2006)

At last an image comes, several tangerines,

in childhood, placed near his hospital bed.

His mother had found them somewhere.

Though his little brother begged one, mother
    refused.

He shared, but neither

would eat the last tangerine,

which stayed on the night stand.

Who knows what became of it ?

So he eats tangerines all winter,

especially on snowy days, gray days.

He eats slowly, as if

there's plenty of time,

as if he's devouring darkness.

He eats, peels, and when he lifts his head,

snow glitters at the window.

(2006) (tr. by Diana Shi and George O'Connell)

吉狄马加 Jidi Majia

吉狄马加(1961-），诗人，彝族，生于四川凉山。现为中国作家协会副主席，在国内外出版诗集 50 余部，包括《一个彝人的梦想》（1990）、《火焰与词语——吉狄马加诗集》（1997）、《群山的影子——吉狄马加诗选》（2014）、《从雪豹到马雅可夫斯基》（2017）等。

Jidi Majia, Chinese poet of *Yi* minority, born in 1961 at Liangshan, Sichuan Province, currently serves as the Vice-chairman of Chinese Writers' Association. He is the author of over 50 poetry books, including, *A Native Yi's Dream*, *Words of Fire——Poems by Jidi Majia*, *Shade of our Mountain Range——Jidi Majia's Selected Poems*, *From the Snow Leopard to Mayakovsky*.

自由 / Freedom

我曾问过真正的智者
什么是自由？
智者的回答总是来自典籍
我以为那就是自由的全部

有一天在那拉提草原
傍晚时分
我看见一匹马
悠闲地走着，没有目的

Once upon a time I asked a truly wise man
What is Freedom ?
The wise man's answers always came from ancient texts
I thought that's all there was to Freedom

Once on the Nalati plain
As night was falling
I saw a horse
Walking slowly, with no aim

一个喝醉了酒的

哈萨克骑手

在马背上酣睡

是的,智者解释的是自由的含义

但谁能告诉我,在那拉提草原

这匹马和它的骑手

谁更自由呢?

And a drunken

Kazakh rider

Who was sleeping soundly on its back

It's true the wise man explained the meaning of freedom

But who could tell me, there on the Nalati plain

Which was freer —

The horse or the rider ?

(tr. by Andrea Lingenfelter)

时间 / Time

在我的故乡	In my hometown
我无法见证	I fail to witness
一道土墙的全部历史	the entire history of an earthen wall
那是因为在一个瞬间	Because at some instant
我无法亲历	I fail to be present
一粒尘埃	When a dust-speck goes through
从诞生到死亡的过程	its whole birth-to-death process
哦，时间！	O, time!
是谁用无形的剪刀	Who uses unseen scissors
在距离和速度的平台	to cut you into pieces
把你剪成了碎片	on the platform of distance and velocity
其实我们	Actually, we needn't wonder
不用问时间的起源	about the origin of time
因为它从来	because there never was
就没有所谓的开始	anything like a beginning to time

同样，我们也不用问	Nor need we wonder
它的归宿在哪里	about its final resting place
因为在浩瀚的宇宙	because in the boundless universe
它等同于无限	it is equal to infinity
时间是黑暗中的心脏	Time is the heart in the dark
它的每一次跳动	Each time it throbs
就如同一道闪电	like a bolt of lightning, it will be
它是过去、现在和未来的桥梁	a bridge joining past, present and future
请相信，这并非上帝的意志	Believe me, none of it is God's will
仿佛是绝对的真理	It seems like the absolute truth
当时间离开了我们	that time will never return
它便永远不再回头	if it gets away from us

所有的生命、思想和遗产	All of life and thought and heritage
都栖居在时间的圣殿	dwell in the temple of time
哦，时间！	O, time !
最为公平的法官	Most impartial judge
它审判谎言	It brings a lie to trial
同时它也伸张正义	while it upholds justice

是它在最终的时刻

改变了一切精神和物质的

存在形式

它永远在死亡中诞生

又永远在诞生中死亡

它包含了一切

它又在一切之外

如果说在这个世界上

有什么东西真正的不朽

我敢肯定地说：那就是时间！

Time in the final moment

changes all existing forms

of spirit and matter

It is ever born from death

and ever dies in birth

It includes everything

and is beyond everything

if there is something

immortal in this world

I would definitely say: it is time!

(tr. by Hai An & Cassandra Atherton)

高兴　Gao Xing

高兴（1963-），诗人，翻译家，出生于江苏吴江，现居北京，《世界文学》主编。
Gao Xing（1963-）, Chinese poet and translator, was born in Wujing, Jiangsu Province in China, currently serving as the Editor-in-Chief of *World Literature* at Beijing.

水鸟

绝没有料到

水面上也会冷不丁地

冒出带着斑纹图案的障碍

这难道是天空投下的幻影

水鸟眨了眨眼

小心翼翼地游近，用喙试了试

又赶紧缩回。该如何是好

该如何是好?水鸟停在水中

琢磨着，迟疑着

Water Bird

Out of the blue,

a streaked obstacle abruptly

emerges from the water.

Or is it a shadow of the sky?

The water bird, blinking,

swims near, taps his beak on it,

suddenly retreats. What shall I do?

What shall I do? The bird stays in the water,

pondering, hesitating,

as if there are three paths before him:

仿佛有三条路摆在面前
折返，潜泳，或者飞翔
三条路，三种可能，三个方向

只见那水鸟先是折返，游了
几步，随后转身，一个猛子
潜入水中，片刻之后又在
障碍的那边，露出头颈
最终奋力一搏，飞了起来
朝向天空，朝向自己所认定的
远方，将三条路变成了一条路
三种可能变成了一种可能
三个方向变成了一个方向

那水鸟才有资格谈论自由
可它却什么也没说

它已什么也不用说了

backtracking, diving, or flying.
Three paths, three possibilities, three directions.

Then the bird goes back, swims

a few strokes, turns around again,

diving into the water. A moment later,

across the obstacle, his head and neck resurface.

Eventually he strives to fly up

toward the sky, toward the horizon

he believes in, turning the three paths,

the three possibilities,

the three directions, all into one.

Only that bird is qualified to talk about freedom.

He says nothing.

There's no need for him to say anything.

(tr. by Liang Yujing)

母亲 / Mother

该添衣裳了
千里之外,母亲说

这句话
母亲已说了几十年
一到秋天,就说
无论我在哪里
无论我多大年龄

像默契,又像仪式
年年,我都等着
母亲说这句话
等着帮母亲,也帮自己
完成一项温暖的事业

每回听到这句话

"Dress more warmly this time of year"
From six hundred miles away my mother says

For decades
She has spoken these words
Every year come autumn
No matter where I am
No matter how many birthdays pass

As if by tacit agreement, or in a ritual
Each year I await
The day for these words to be spoken
So I can help Mother and myself
To fulfill this gesture of warm feeling

Each time I hear these words

我都会眼眶一热

都会忘掉所有的言语

只是不住地点头：晓得了，晓得了

A stinging warmth fills my eyes

As I forget all other language

Except to nod and say," I know, I know"

(tr. by Denis Mair)

汪剑钊　Wang Jianzhao

汪剑钊（1963–），诗人、翻译家，生于浙江湖州，现为北京外国语大学教授，著有诗文集《诗歌的乌鸦时代》等。
Wang Jianzhao, Chinese poet and translator, born in 1963 at Huzhou, Zhejiang Province, currently the Professor at Beijing International Studies University. He is the author of several poetry book including *The Crow Era of Poetry*.

比永远多一秒　　　　　　　　A Second More Than Forever

一片啼啭的云飘过，
遮住摩天大楼的避雷针，
而我，把你肉感的短消息握在掌心，
仿佛怀抱一个盛大的节日。

我随手整理了一下身上的红毛衣，
超现实地联想到艾吕雅，
自由之手曾经疯狂地建造爱情的水晶屋。
一项必须两个人完成的事业：

A singing cloud floats by,
Masking the lightning rods of skyscrapers,
I hold your sensual message in my palm,
As if embracing a grand festival.

I tidy up my red sweater conveniently,
Making a surreal association with Paul Eluard,
Whose liberty hand once crazily built the crystal house of love.
A career must be accomplished by two persons:

生活，赶在终点站消失之前，
我无可救药地爱你，
那是情感专列对于时间钢轨的迷恋，
永远爱你，永远……

哦，不，比永远还要多出一秒！

(2012)

A life is done, before the terminal fades away,

I love you irredeemably,

It is an infatuation, an emotional train on a time rail,

Always I love you, always……

Oh, no, a second more than forever!

(2012)

初春是冬天的一个伤口

铁屋——窗扇打开如一对翅膀，

瞎子凭借耳朵觉察到意外。

空气涌动，秘密传递着流言：

春天是冬天的一个伤口，

裸露跨越世纪的疼痛。

这是死亡与诞生共存的时间。

厂洼路的雪水流淌，坚硬

成为过去，柔软已成为时尚。

泥泞，随暮色一起降临，

布满黑白相间的棋盘。

一棵树在默哀，另一棵树在沙哑地

歌唱，无知的幼芽费力地

钻出地层，期待一棵青草

或一枝玫瑰的命运，

期待绿色的光。

An Early Spring Is a Wound in Winter

An iron house opens its window as a pair of wings,

A blind man perceives an accident by ear.

The wind rises, passing on the rumor in secret:

An early spring, a wound in winter,

Bares its pain across the centuries.

It is the time for death and birth to coexist.

The snow turns to slush on the Changwa road

None harder than before, but it's soft in a fashion.

So muddy, in the gathering dusk of evening,

As a board full of black and white.

One tree is in silence, the other is singing in a hoarse tone

An innocent bud emerges from the ground

Looking forward to the fate

Of green grass or of a rose,

Awaiting the green light.

The wind blows from afar,

风,隐蔽地从远方吹来,

比月光更尖锐。

寒意像一只黑鸟,

撞击万泉河峭立的冰凌,

羽毛纷飞,

如一束乌亮的针刺。

初春,把冬天的伤口打开……

(2008)

Sharper than the moonlight.

A chill, like a black bird,

Hits the icy ice along the Wanquan River,

Feathers fluttering

Like a bunch of bright needles.

An early spring, opens the wound in winte

(2008)(tr. by Hai An & Cassandra Atherton)

树才 Shu Cai

树才（1965–），诗人、翻译家，生于浙江奉化，现居北京。出版有诗集《单独者》《树才短诗选》等。
Shu Cai, Chinese poet and translator, was born in 1965 at Fenghua, Zhejiang Province, currently lives in Beijing. He is the author of several poetry books including *A Loner* and *Selected Short Poems By Shu Cai*.

莲花

我盘腿打坐度过了

许多宁静无望的暗夜。

我呼吸着人的一吐一纳——

哦，世界？它几乎不存在。

另一个世界存在……

另一些风，另一些牺牲的羔羊，

另一些面孔，但也未必活生生……

总之，它们属于另一个空间。

Lotus

I have spent many tranquil and desireless nights

Sitting with my legs crossed in meditation.

I breathe a human's breath—in and out—

Eh, world? It hardly exists.

Another world exists…

Other winds, other sacrificial lambs,

Other faces, not necessarily lively…

In other words, they belong to another space.

打开的双掌，是我仅有的两朵莲花。

你说它们生长，但朝哪个方向？

你说它们赶路，但想抵达哪里？

我只是在学习遗忘——

好让偌大的宇宙不被肉眼瞥见。

(1994)

I spread my hands, the only two lotuses I own.

You say they are growing—but in what direction?

You say they are on their way—but where to reach?

I'm merely learning to forget—

Let that huge universe be unseen by eyes of flesh.

(1994) (tr. by Leonard Schwartz & Zhang Er)

安宁　　　　　　　　　　　Tranquility

我想写出此刻的安宁	I want to write this moment's tranquility
我心中枯草一样驯服的安宁	my inner tranquility like a humble dried grass
被风吹送着一直升向天庭的安宁	the tranquility flying to the heavens in the wind
我想写出这住宅小区的安宁	I want to write this neighborhood's tranquility
汽车开走了停车场空荡荡的安宁	the empty tranquility in the parking lot after all the cars have gone
儿童们奔跑奶奶们闲聊的安宁	the tranquility of grandmas chatting while the kids running
我想写出这风中的清亮的安宁	I want to write a clean and bright tranquility in this wind
草茎颤动着咝咝响的安宁	the rushing tranquility of shivering grass
老人裤管里瘦骨的安宁	the skinny tranquility in the trousers of an old man
我想写出这泥地上湿乎乎的安宁	I want to write the wet tranquility of the earth
阳光铺出的淡黄色的安宁	the yellowish tranquility spread by sunshine
断枝裂隙间干巴巴的安宁	the dry tranquility among the broken twigs
我想写出这树影笼罩着的安宁	I want to write the tranquility under the shadow of a tree
以及树影之外的安宁	and the tranquility beyond the shadow
以及天地间青蓝色的安宁	and the blue and greenish tranquility between sky and earth
我这么想着没工夫再想别的	Thus thinking, I have no time to think of other things

我这么想着一路都这么想着

占据我全身心的，就是这

——安宁

(2000)

Thus thinking, I think of this all the way

It is just the tranquility which

occupied my mind

(2000) (tr. by Leonard Schwartz & Gao Xing)

车前子 Che Qianzi

车前子（1963— ），诗人、画家，生于江苏苏州，现居北京。出版有诗集《纸梯》《怀抱公鸡的素食者》（英文版）及散文集多部。

Che Qianzi (1963–), born in Suzhou, Jiangsu Province, is currently living as a poet and Painter in Beijing. He is the author of several collections of poetry and essay including *Paper Ladder* and *A Vegetarian Carrying a Rooster in his Arms*.

无诗歌（选章）

我们是蛮族，

只有一个妻子，

早已离婚。

*

刮来大群燕子，

小城简陋（抽搐的电线之上，

黏着一只又一只破烂纸袋，

纸袋中，装着剪刀。）

No Poetry (excerpts)

We are barbarians,

with only one wife,

long divorced.

*

A flock of swallows,

In a simple town (stuck on twitching wires,

torn paper bags, one after another,

inside each, a pair of scissors.)

*

她没有疯!

领卡夫卡回家过夜,

是想验证——

明早床上的《昆虫记》。

第二天,一堆小人,

数也数不清,

在被窝里。

*

She's not crazy!

taking Kafka home for the night,

trying to verify—

the metamorphose in bed on the morning.

The next day, a crowd of dwarves,

numerous,

under the quilt.

宇宙

最后,夏天敲打了小石子。

拉过一条长凳,让我坐下。

此院,突然得,

从不作声,

低头,

闲置,并行——

闲置一棵并行的灰色的苹果树。

Cosmos

At last, summer knocks with a pebble.

Grab a bench and let me sit down.

Suddenly, in this courtyard,

Always quiet,

Head lowered,

Idle, parallel—

Idle and parallel to a gray apple tree.

(tr. by Huang Yunte)

李少君　Li Shaojun

李少君 (1967–)，诗人，湖南人，现为《诗刊》副主编，出版有诗集《蓝吧》《那些消失了的人》《岛》等。
Li Shaojun, Chinese poet, born in 1967 in Hunan, currently serves as the vice chief-editor of *Poetry* magazine in Beijing. He is the author of several poetry books including *Blue Bar*, *Those Who Disappear* and *Island*.

四合院

一座四合院，浮在秋天的花影里
夜晚，桂花香会浸入熟睡者的梦乡
周围，全是熟悉的亲人
——父母、姐姐、妹妹
都在静静地安睡

那曾经是我作为一个游子
漂泊在异乡时最大的梦想

A *Sihe* Courtyard

A *Sihe* Courtyard, emerges from flower shadows in autumn
At night, the fragrance of sweet osmanthus infuses the dreams of sound sleepers
All around are the familiar relatives
—parents and sisters
all in sound sleep

This is my greatest dream of a traveler
Who roves over a strange land

流水

每次,她让我摸摸乳房就走了
我在我手上散发的她的体香中
迷离恍惚,并且回味荡漾
我们很长时间才见一次面
一见面她就使劲掐我
让我对生活还保持着感觉
知道还有痛,还有伤心
她带我去酒吧,在包厢里
我唱歌,她跳艳舞
然后用手机拍下艳照再删除
我们最强烈的一次发作是去深山中
远离尘世,隔绝人间
我们差点想留下来不走了
可是她不肯跟我做爱
只让我看她的赤身裸体,百媚千娇
她让我摸摸她的乳房就抽身而去

Running Water

Each time she allows me to feel her breast and goes
  away
Her lingering scent on my hands
makes me bewildered, and is a impressive fragrance
We have a date at long intervals
She pinches me painfully when she sees me
and keeps me sensible to life
to pain, at least to sorrows
She brings me to bars
singing and dancing naked in the box
then takes and deletes amorous photos in her cell
  phone
Our most impressive moments took place deep in
  the mountains
Far from the world, isolated from the world
We almost reside there
but she is unwilling to make love with me
merely allowing me to watch her naked body, fresh

随后她会发来大量短信

"亲爱的,开心点,我喜欢你笑"

"这次心情不好,下次好好补偿你"

"我会想你的,再见!"

我承认我一直没琢磨透她

她孤身一人在外,却又守身如玉

这让我为她担心,甚至因此得了轻度抑郁症

而她仍笑靥如花,直到有一天

她乘地铁出门,将自己沉入水底

随流水远去,让我再也找她不到

and charming

merely allowing me to feel her breast before she goes away

Then she sends me many messages

"Honey, cheer up, I love you, love your smile"

"In a bad mood today, make up for it next time"

"I'll miss you, bye-bye!"

I admit that I have not figured her out

Living alone away from home, yet she keeps herself as pure as jade

It makes me worried about her, even slightly depressed

but she still smiles as a flower, until one day

she goes out by the subway, drowning herself in the water

Gone with running water, she is inaccessible to me forever

(tr. by Hai An & Cassandra Atherton)

周瓒 Zhou Zan

周瓒（1968–），诗人，江苏人，现供职于中国社会科学院文学研究所。出版诗集《松开》《哪吒的另一重生活》等。
Zhou Zan, Chinese poet, born in 1968 in Jiangsu Province, currently works at the Literature Institute, Chinese Academy of Social Science in Beijing. She is the author of several poetry books including *Unclasp* and *Nazhe's Another Life*.

翼 / Wings

有着旗帜的形状，但她们

从不沉迷于随风飘舞

她们的节拍器（谁的发明？）

似乎专门用来抗拒风的方向

显然，她们有自己隐秘的目标。

当她们长在我们躯体的暗处

（哦，去他的风车的张扬癖！）

她们要用有形的弧度，对称出

飞禽与走兽的差别

though shaped like banners, the women

never indulge in dancing in the wind,

their metronome (who invented it ?)

seems to be set mainly to resist the wind's direction,

obviously they have their own, hidden objective.

when they grow in the hidden parts of our bodies

(oh, that blasted windmill's weakness for public spectacle!)

they must use a curved form, to bring out symmetrically

the difference between the birds and the beasts;

(not including angels and bats)

（天使和蝙蝠不包括于其中）
假如她们的意志发展成一项
事业，好像飞行也是
一种生活或维持生活的手段
她们会意识到平衡的必要
但所有的旗帜都不在乎
这一点；而风筝
安享于摇头摆尾的快乐。
当羽翼丰满，躯体就会感到
一种轻逸，如同正从内部
鼓起了一个球形的浮漂
因而，一条游鱼的羽翅
决非退化的小摆设，它仅意味着
心的自由必须对称于水的流动

if their will develops into a

cause, like flying also is

a way of living or a means of supporting life,

they will realize the need for balance,

but not a single banner cares the least about

this point, and kites

content themselves with complacent happiness

when wings are full, the bodies will feel

a kind of ease and freedom, like a ball-shaped buoy

that comes from within and swells outward;

thus, the fins of a swimming fish

are by no means retrogressive ornament, but merely imply that

the heart's freedom must be symmetrical to the flow of the water.

(tr. by Steve Riep)

致一位诗人,我的同行

给你的诗必须是这样一种体式
两行平行,仿佛我们并肩走在街上

这也意味着,停顿,是在谈话中
转折,就像话题转弯,拐往另一条街

慢,是我们心仪的速度,但也不能
变成一种自我暗示,甚至借口,所以沉默

是的,很久以来我们都互相沉默
就算我们一起走过相同的路,进过同一家馆子

今天,我们有一个明确的目的
你领我去一个地方,如果我选择了跟随

那将意味着:我不再沉默,我需要一个出口
就算我们进入的,是那先行者们都曾领受过的
　　炼狱

For a Poet, My Confrere

A poem for you must be in this form,
in parallel couplets, like we're strolling shoulder-to-shoulder

This also means that a pause is a turn in conversation,
like a change in topic, turning onto another street

We admire a slow pace, but this must not
become a self-hinting, an excuse even, therefore silence

Yes, for a long time we've been silent to each other
though we've walked the same road, entered the same
　　restaurant

Today, we have a definite purpose
you'll lead me to a place, if I choose to follow

This will mean: I won't be silent, I'll need an exit
though we're entering the purgatory of our forbearers

(tr. by Eleanor Goodman & Wang Ao)

周瑟瑟　Zhou Sese

周瑟瑟(1968–)，诗人，小说家，生于湖南，现居北京。出版有诗集《17年——周瑟瑟诗选》《松树下：周瑟瑟编年诗选》等。

Zhou Sese, Chinese poet and novelist, born in 1968 in Hunan, currently lives in Beijing. He is the author of several poetry books of *17 Years——Selected Poems of Zhou Sese* and *Under Pine Tree: Selected Chronicle Poems of Zhou Sese*.

人群中总有一个好看的

There Will Always Be a Nice-looking Girl in the Crowd

人群中总有一个好看的

她因为长着一张鹿脸

一眼就认出了她

人群中还有另一个好看的

他的风衣领竖着

他的身形轮廓与人群区别开来

在时代的人群中

总会冒出与时代格格不入的人

There will always be a nice-looking girl in the crowd

She's got a deer face

recognized at first glance

There will always be another nice-looking man in the crowd

his wind coat's collar upright

his figure distinct from the crowd

In the crowd of the day

大部分人神态自若

而他们略显紧张

生动的面孔

保留了动物的特征

警觉、羞愧、自尊

这样的人

如星星之火忽闪忽闪

又像特务一样出现在人群中

长筒彩色条纹袜

与白色球鞋搭配

她转头，哦，她转过头

在人群中寻找

另一个好看的人

(2016)

there always appears some people out of place

Most people look perfectly calm

but they're a bit nervous

A vivid face

preserves an animal's feature

alert, blushed in his self-respect

Such a man

flashing as as park

appears in the crowd as a spy

Long-stockings in color stripe

matched with white sneakers

She turns around, oh, she turns around

looking for another nice-looking man

in the crowd

(2016)

另一种爱

用铁栏把小区包起来
再在铁栏上绣花
我生活在里面
与我的亲人
一起生活在铁栏里
我们没有感觉到
铁栏的压力
有时我把铁栏看作
是另一种爱
它爱我的温顺
也爱我的倔强
我有时候把头
猛地插进铁栏间
我头上的鲜血
染红了铁栏
与铁栏上的花朵

Another Kind of Love

Wrap up the block with an iron railing

then embroider on the railing

I am living behind iron railings

together with my family

behind the iron railings

We never feel

the pressure of iron railings

Sometimes I take the railings

as another kind of love

The railings love my meekness

and love my stubbornness as well

Sometimes I plunge my head in

between the iron railings

The railing and its flowers

stained with the blood

of my head

那片刻

钻心的疼痛

让我哇哇大哭

我知道这正是

另一种爱

At that moment

the burning pain

makes me cry

I know it's just

another kind of love

(2016)(tr. by Hai An & Cassandra Atherton)

翟永明　Zhai Yongming

翟永明（1955-），诗人，四川成都人。出版诗集《女人》《在一切玫瑰之上》《翟永明诗集》《黑夜里的素歌》《称之为一切》等。

Zhai Yongming, Chinese poetess, was born in 1955 at Chengdu, Sichuan Province. She is the author of several poetry books including *Woman, Above all Roses, Poems by Zhai Yongming, Simple Songs of Night* and *Call It Everything*.

渴望

今晚所有的光只为你照亮
今晚你是一小块殖民地
久久停留，忧郁从你身体内
渗出，带着细腻的水滴

月亮像一团光洁芬芳的肉体
酣睡，发出诱人的气息
两个白昼夹着一个夜晚
在它们之间，你黑色眼圈

Desire

Tonight all the lights are shining for you
Tonight you are a small colonial outpost
You've lingered long here, and melancholy seeps out
From your body, with tiny, perfect drops of water

Like a clean bright ball of scented flesh, the moon
Sleeps sweetly, each breath a seduction
One night squeezed between two days
And in their midst, the black orbs of your eyes

保持着欣喜

怎样的喧嚣堆积成我的身体
无法安慰,感到有某种物体将形成
梦中的墙壁发黑
使你看见三角形泛滥的影子
全身每个毛孔都张开
不可捉摸的意义
星星在夜空毫无人性地闪耀
而你的眼睛装满
来自远古的悲哀和快意

带着心满意足的创痛
你优美的注视中,有着恶魔的力量
使这一刻,成为无法抹掉的记忆

Still filled with joy

What sort of noises were raked together to make my body
Inconsolable, feeling like some sort of substance was about to t
 take shape
The walls in the dream turn black
Showing you the shadows of a flood of triangles
Every pore on your body opens wide
Concepts you can't grasp
Stars in the night sky glimmer inhumanly
But your eyes are brimming
With the sorrows and joys of antiquity

Bearing the wounds of perfect contentment
Your beautiful gaze has a demonic power
Making this moment a memory that can never be erased

独白   Monologue

我，一个狂想，充满深渊的魅力	I, this fantasy, profoundly enchanting
偶然被你诞生。泥土和天空	Happened to be borne by you. Soil and sky
二者合一，你把我叫作女人	Combining into one, you called me woman
并强化了我的身体	And strengthened my body
我是软得像水的白色羽毛体	I'm a white feather as soft as water
你把我捧在手上，我就容纳这个世界	You hold me in your hands, and I contain this world
穿着肉体凡胎，在阳光下	Clothed in this mortal flesh, standing in the sunlight
我是如此炫目，使你难以置信	I am so dazzling, you can hardly believe
我是最温柔最懂事的女人	I am the gentlest and wisest of women
看穿一切却愿分担一切	Seeing through everything, yet wanting to share in all burdens
渴望一个冬天，一个巨大的黑夜	Longing for a winter, an immense dark night
以心为界，我想握住你的手	In the world of the heart, I want to grasp your hand
但在你的面前我的姿态就是一种惨败	But in your eyes my posture is utterly defeated

当你走时,我的痛苦

要把我的心从口中呕出

用爱杀死你,这是谁的禁忌

太阳为全世界升起!我只为了你

以最仇恨的柔情蜜意贯注你全身

从脚至顶,我有我的方式

一片呼救声,灵魂也能伸出手

大海作为我的血液就能把我

高举到落日脚下,有谁记得我

但我所记得的,绝不仅仅是一生

When you went away, I nearly spit out

My heart in grief

To kill you with love, who says that's forbidden

The sun rises for the entire world! But only for you do I

Fix my vengeful tenderness on your body

From head to toe, after my own fashion

Cries for help all around, can the soul extend a hand?

If the sea were my blood then it might

Raise me up to the feet of the setting sun, but who would remember me?

But what I remember, is more than just one life

(tr. by Andrea Lingenfelter)

张烨　Zhang Ye

张烨，诗人，上海人，上海大学文学院教授。著有诗集《诗人之恋》（1986）《鬼男》（英汉对照，2004）《隔着时空凝望》（2015）及散文集《孤独是一支天籁》等。

Zhang Ye, Chinese poet, born in Shanghai, Professor of Literature at Shanghai University. She has published widely both as a poet and as an essay writer, including *Poet's Love* (1986) and *Ghost Man* (2004).

忘川①

我的心，浸泡在最恐怖的时刻

忘了悲伤，像一双麻木的脚

到处踩着虚空

沙砾击面

狂风将冥河吹得翻黑翻白

一头紫金色的蛇人在水中央歌唱

"我的歌声是芬芳的乙醚，溶在水里

---

①忘川，即冥府之河。鬼魂在进入冥府之前，必须饮此河之水，饮此水后能忘记尘世的一切。

The River Lethe

My heart, soaked in a time of terror,

Has forgotten sorrow, and its numbed feet

Plod far and wide through the unreal.

Pebbles sting my face, the wind

Lashes the Styx into a black and white turmoil.

Purple and gold, a snake figure stings from the river.

"My singing makes the fragments ether, dissolved in water.

People, you must drink of the waters of Lethe.

人啊，你必将喝忘川之水

这里充满残酷、腐败、堕落、卑鄙

没有希望没有理想没有梦幻

浪漫主义是最虚伪的东西

让惬意的忘川充满你的灵魂吧

  你将永远无忧无虑

  人啊，你必将喝忘川之水

  有的水为干渴而喝

  有的水却为不得不喝

    喝吧，喝吧

    我的歌声是芬芳的乙醚

    溶在水里……"

歌声牵引我们昏昏然走向忘川

三千双手同时捧起河水

蛇人带着阴险的微笑消失在水面

"复仇者，你不能忘记过去……"

一个绝望的声音像泗水者在惊涛中呐喊

抒月，我的情人，你急切的声音

Here corruption lives, ruthlessness, depravity and avarice.

Here there is no hope, no vision, no dream.

Love is diluted, becomes the greatest lie.

Let the soothing Lethe fill your souls

  And empty them of trouble.

  People, you must drink of the waters of Lethe.

  Some waters assuage thirst,

  Others minister to a greater need.

    Drink…drink…

    My song is fragrant ether,

    Dissolved in water…"

The singing leads us, drowsily, to Lethe.

Three thousands pairs of hands together cup the water.

The snake figure, with a knowing smile, disappears.

"Avenger, you can't forget the past…"

A despairing voice, like that of a drowning swimmer.

穿凿这里的世界

沿着缠树的枯藤爬向我耳边

低声有力地说：乐，你不能忘掉我！"

我艰难地将手指捅进喉管：一连串呕吐

阴雾舔着我的泪，我站立，同远山对峙

河水以平静的心情缓缓流动

流过我的足踝

流过三千鬼魂丧失了记忆的睡眠

我突然迸发一阵狂笑

无可拯救的声音在死亡的世界回荡

Shūyuè, lover, your anxious voice,

Forcing its way through this world,

Climbs to me along withered vines on the trees,

Telling me, softly, forcefully: "Lè, you cannot forget me!"

I ram my fingers down my throat and retch, again and again.

The mist licks my tears. I face the distant mountains.

The river flows slowly, quietly by,

Flows over my ankles,

Flows past three thousands ghosts, sleeping without memory.

All at once I shriek with laughter. My voice

Echoes beyond salvation in the world of the dead.

骷髅舞

我们，又脏又臭，是一群恶毒的狞笑，
将拧紧的地狱旋开，将巨创的灵魂释放
让僵死的欢乐复苏
记忆中的空气多么清新
恋人的爱心又是多么坚定
无休止的悒闷以后，需要补偿
来吧，漂亮的骷髅！让我们
欢歌、狂舞、嬉笑
  "我的时代还没有到来
   有的人死后方生"①

磷火飞旋，棺木噼啪，碎片凌空
像打击磐石一样狠狠打击自己
合唱四起：忧狮、忧虎、悲狐、哀猿

---

① "我的时代还没有到来 / 有的人死后方生"出自《尼采选集》第 2 卷第 429 页。

Skeleton Dance

Stinking, filthy, we are a troupe of evil smiles,
Unscrewing the gates of hell, releasing wounded souls,
Leading the dead in a merry new dance,
The air in the memory quickens into freshness,
The lover's heart again is constant,
Long suffering cries out for recompense,
Come, you beautiful skeletons. Let's sing.
Like mad, dance like mad! Let's party!
My time has not yet come
Some are born after death ①

Phosphorescence whirls, coffins splinter towards the sky.
We flail ourselves as if we were smiting a rock.
Our dried-up feet begin to find a rhythm.
Everywhere the renewed chorus rises: lions, tigers, foxes, apes,
We stretch our voices that had been frozen and burnt into

---

① "My time has not yet come; some are born posthumously." - Friedrich Nietzsche, *Ecce Homo*.

我们张大冷得溃烂、烧得焦臭的嗓门

来吧，阿幸让我们旋转

我要帮助你恢复记忆

一具骷髅紧搂着一具骷髅

白骨孳生血肉的欲望

我演奏月亮

指骨践踏一连串半音阶琴键

旋律怪诞、戏谑、死的愉快、死的辉煌

眼睛，两个空洞窀穸，扁平的鼻孔

通往地狱，死色的疯狂是一种超级舞姿

俯身为零度仇

俯面为沸点恨

生者无常死者也无常

一切思维无力抵达未知的境域

活着时谁在冥冥中操纵我们的命运

生命既然无谜可猜

死亡既然难以诠释

foulness,

Come, A Xing, let us spin and spin

Let me spin you back into remembering.

Skeletons cling to one to another,

Bones stirring like flesh and blood

I play the moon, like music,

My bony fingers rattle up and down the scale,

A strange, dramatic music, energised by death.

My eyes are empty graves, my bare flattened nostrils,

Are entrances to hell. Death-hued madness energises the dance:

Look down and hatred disappears,

Look up and it boils above your head.

The living do not endure, nor do the dead.

Mind alone will not attain the realm beyond knowledge.

Who can influence the darker future of the still living ?

那么，我模糊扭曲的舞姿想要表达什么
整部灵魂是一种苍凉的感知

叮咚……我爱抒月，我演奏抒月
抒月之声在地狱交响
一具骷髅紧搂着一具骷髅
舞啊，不生不灭，不灭不生
喧阗着无声之声
喧阗着红蒙蒙的混沌初开
白茫茫一片终结
欢乐啊，天下人间
欢乐啊，碧落黄泉

Since life's riddles are beyond guessing,

Since death also is beyond explanation,

What is the meaning of this strange, distorted
   dance?

My soul is infused with emptiness.

Bell music…I love Shū yuè, I play Shūyuè like music.

Shūyuè's voice rings around this hell.

Skeletons embrace one another.

The dance shimmers in and out of vision.

There is a sound that is beyond sound.

Chaos utters a red, primal cry and is silent

In a great expanse of white

Human happiness in the sky

Stretching towards the earth.

(tr. by Gabriel Rosenstock & Yu Jiànzhōng)

王寅　Wang Yin

王寅（1962-），诗人，上海人，20世纪80年代"海上诗群"代表人物。出版有《王寅诗选》《摄手记》《灰光灯》等。
Wang Yin, Chinese poet, born in 1962 in Shanghai, was the representative poet of *"At Sea* poetry group" in the 1980s, publishing several books including *Selected Poems by Wang Yin, Photo Notes* and *Grey Light*.

白色的海洋　　　　　　　　White Sea

白色的海洋穿过黎明的医院

裸露的玻璃尚有余温

我躺在冰冷的人行道上

水泥地面像镜子一样冰冷，城市

在我的脊柱之下

无声无息地运行

在悲伤的底层

不是夜晚又能是什么

A white sea courses through the hospital before
　dawn

Traces of warmth lingering on naked glass

I lie on the ice-cold sidewalk

Its concrete surface frozen as a mirror, the city

Beneath my spine

Running on silently

In the lowest depths of pain

It can only be night

我的沉睡唤作沉睡

我的哭泣是所有的哭泣

抒情的润滑剂

打开谎言的盖子

宇宙这样一朽

青春无可怀疑

白色的海洋穿过黎明的医院

轻盈的钢铁叙述着

锈蚀已久的夏天

My sleep bears the name of all deep sleep

My tears are all of the tears there are

The balm of lyricism

Lifts the lid on lies

The universe is so easily broken

Youth knows no doubts

A white sea courses through the hospital before
   dawn

While supple steel gives an account

Of a summer long fallen into rust

晚年来得太晚了

晚年来得太晚了
在不缺少酒的时候
已经找不到杯子，夜晚
再也没有了葡萄的颜色

十月的向日葵是昏迷的雨滴
也是燃烧的绸缎
放大了颗粒的时间
装满黑夜的相册

漂浮的草帽遮盖着
隐名埋姓的风景
生命里的怕、毛衣下的痛
风暴聚集了残余的灵魂

晚年来得太晚了

The Evening of My Life Has Come Too Late

The evening of my life has come too late

There's wine in abundance

But no cups to be found, and nightfall

Has drained the grapes of their color

October sunflowers are drunken raindrops

Smoldering silks and satins

Magnified particles of time

Filling the photo album of night

Bobbing straw hats block out

A landscape that's going under cover

The fear in life, the soreness under a sweater

A storm gathers in all of the leftover souls

我继续遵循爱与死的预言

一如我的心早就

习惯了可耻的忧伤

The evening of my life has come too late

I still abide by the prophecies of Love and Death

Just as my heart long ago

Became inured to grief and its shame

(tr. by Andrea Lingenfelter)

陈东东　Chen Dongdong

陈东东（1961–），诗人，上海人，20世纪80年代"海上诗群"代表人物。出版诗集《海神的一夜》《明净的部分》《即景与杂说》《解禁书》，混合文本《流水》《下扬州》等。

Chen Dongdong, Chinese poet, born in 1961 in Shanghai, was the representative poet of "*At Sea* poetry group" in the 1980s. He is the author of several poetry books including *One Night of the Sea God, The Transparent Part, Ramblings Inspired by These Surroundings, Unbanned Book, Running Water* (Hybrid Text) and *Down to Yangzhou*.

莫名镇 / Unnamed Town

一条河在此转折

就已经造就了它

何况还有

两岸水泥栏杆的粗陋

剥落绿色的邮政建筑也足以

构成它

　　再加上两三棵树

荫阴里停着大钢圈自行车

The bend here in the river

has made it what it is

and even more so

the crudeness of the cement railings on both banks

The postal building with peeling green is enough to

　form it

　　along with two or three trees

under whose shade is a steel-wheeled bicycle

The small bank is a necessary facility

小银行则是必要的设施

玻璃门蒙尘，映现对街

蒙尘的学校

　　　广播在广播

广播体操反复地广播

另一些影子属于几个人

不愿意稍稍挪动自己

在桥上低头看流水

在家庭旅馆的椭圆形院子里

看一盘残棋浮出深井

百货铺。菜市场。剃头店

网吧幽暗因为从前那是个谷仓

从电脑显示屏颤抖的对话框

到来者跨出，来到了此地

他其实不想找在此要找的，正当

这么个时刻……这么个时代

(2010)

with glass doors covered in dust, setting off the dust-
　　covered school across the street and the broadcaster
　　broadcasting
a broadcast exercise routine on repeated broadcast

The other shadows belongs to a few people
who don't want to move at all
on the bridge they look down into the river
and in the oval courtyard at their guesthouse
they watch a Go board emerge from a well

Convenience stores. Vegetable markets. Barbershops
an internet café dim because it once was a granary
and a visitor steps out
of the chat box on the computer screen, and arrives here
he doesn't want to find what he's looking for here, here in
this moment…this age

(2010)

它仍是一个奇异的词

我知道这邪恶的点滴时间
———狄兰·托马斯

它仍是一个奇异的词

竭力置身于更薄的词典

指向它那不变的所指

它小于种子,重于震颤着

碾来的坦克,它冷于

烫手的火焰一夜凝成冰

它的颜色跟遗忘混同

它依然在,没有被删除

夕阳底下,又一片

覆盖大地的水泥广场上

怀念拾穗的人们弯着腰

并非不能够将它辨认

It's Still a Strange Word

I know this viciousminute's hour
—Dylan Thomas

It's still a strange word

struggling to place itself in a thinner dictionary

it points to its unchanging essence

Small as a seed, weightier

than the quavering of a crushing tank

colder than a scorching flame turning to ice overnight

its color merges with forgetting

It's still there, it hasn't been omitted

under the setting sun, another

cement square that covers the earth

those who think fondly of gleaning bend down

and it's not that they can't identify it

It has never grown, never even sprouted

它从未生长，甚至不发芽

它只愿成为当初喊出的

同一个词，挤破岩壳直坠地心

拖曳着所有黑昼和白夜

它不晦暗，也不是

一个燃烧的词

依然匿藏于更薄的词典

足够被一张纸严密地裹住

它不发亮，也不反射

它缠绕自身的乌有

之光如扭曲铁丝

而当纸的捆绑松开

锈迹斑斑的铁丝刺破

它仍是一个奇异的词

(2014)

it only wants to become the word

that used to be shouted, breaking through mantle
    straight to the core

towing black days and white nights behind it

It isn't dark, and it isn't

a burning word

still hiding in a thinner dictionary

a piece of paper can wrap it up tightly

It doesn't shine, or reflect

it wraps itself around its own nonexistent light

like twisted iron wire

But when the restraints of paper loosen

pierced by the rusty iron wire

It's still a strange word

(2014)(tr. by Eleanor Goodman)

海岸　Hai An

海岸（1965-），诗人，翻译家，浙江台州人，现供职于复旦大学外文学院。出版有诗集《海岸诗选》《挽歌》（长诗）等。

Hai An, Chinese poet and translator, born in 1965 at Taizhou, Zhejiang Province, currently works at the Fudan University. He is the author of several poetry books including *Selected Poems by Hai An, Elegy, A Therapeutic Long Poem*.

灯塔　　　　　　　　　　　Lighthouse

冬夜的江岸无声，少有人外出

我独自在梦境阅读家园

蓦然抬手触及天堂，即

一束光明源自你，灯塔

刺破夜色的光，因尘埃而飞翔

遮住整个航道及飞虫

即刻包容万象，抚慰心灵

恒远的思虑略显沉重

A silent winter evening on the riverbank, with few people about

Completely alone, I dreamily recall my homeland

And suddenly reaching out my hand, touch heaven:

A beam of light appears from the lighthouse !

The light penetrating the darkness, flies in the dust

And covers the river channel and winged insects

It encircles everything and quiets my soul

宁静的航线一侧

停着一条收帆的船队，桅杆

犹如激情燃尽的残骸

无暇顾及你的视线

它们已到达商业，抵达目的地

我淹没在人流中，险象环生

奔腾的流水无处可攀

手臂只想努力挥动：

"灯塔，在这，能看见吗？"

我能看见你，灯塔，如此的幸福

触摸你的光芒更是一种奢华

而另一种奢望，便是进入内部

点燃内心的黑暗，你我的自身

(2001)

And my endless contemplation turns calm

Along the quiet shipping route

Is berthed a row of ships at half-mast

Like bones that have burned up their passion

They take no notice of your glance

Having reached their destination

I drown in the crowds, beset with danger

There is no way to escape the flow

I just want to try to wave:

"Hey, lighthouse, can you see me？"

I am so happy to see you, lighthouse

And get to touch your light

I wish I could go inside you

And light up that inner darkness, yours and mine！

(2001)(tr. by Eleanor Goodman with Hai An)

茶树
——献给好果园

终究入了山林，不再独自漫步
目光迷离于湖的西岸
茶树止住十二月的萧瑟
暖暖的冬青

问茶亦问溪，且行且近
喜乐，一场盼望的寂静
茶香漫无边际
隔季的风景

蛇形的树根下有原罪的气息
风骤起，冬日的雾霾
一枚果子落入幽暗
无名的忧伤

严冬不肃杀，何以见阳春

Tea Bushes
—For an Orchard

Finally entering the mountain forest, no longer
   rambling alone
My eyes blur on the lake's western shore
The tea bushes put an end to December's rustling
A warm wintergreen

Greeting the tea bushes and the brook, walking
   further
Toward joy, yearning for silence
Brimming with the fragrance of tea
And the landscape of a changing season

Beneath serpentine roots is the odor of original sin
The wind howls in the winter haze
A piece of fruit falls into the darkness

一盏灯蓦然睁开了眼

光芒伸出明亮的手

搂紧园里的一切

谁与我们同行,救赎与恩典

日子近了,快让灵魂跟上脚步

(2016)

Laden with nameless sadness

Winter isn't so desolate, and how do we see the
springtime

A lamp suddenly flares to life

The light reaches out its bright arms

To embrace everything in the garden

Come along with us toward salvation and grace

The day draws near, and the soul must keep a
hurried pace

(2016)(tr. by David Perry with Hai An)

梁晓明 Liang Xiaoming

梁晓明 (1963-)，诗人，生于杭州，"北回归线"诗群创始人。出版诗集《用小号把冬天全身吹亮》《印迹——梁晓明组诗和长诗》等。

Liang Xiaoming, Chinese poet, was born in 1963 at Hangzhou, Zhejiang Province. He was the founder of poetry group named as *Tropic of Capricorn*, publishing several poetry books including *Blowing the Winter Bright with a Trumpet* and *Imprint: Liang Xiaoming's Group Poem and Long Poem*.

玻璃 / Glass

我把我的手掌放在玻璃的边刃上
我按下手掌
我把我的手掌顺着这条破边刃
深深往前推

刺骨锥心的疼痛，我咬紧牙关
血，鲜红鲜红的血流下来

顺着破玻璃的边刃

I put my palm on the sharp edge of glass,
I press my palm down
I push my palm forward deeply
along the broken edge

I clench my teeth to the piercing pain
As crimson red blood drips down

Along the sharp edge of broken glass

我一直往前推我的手掌	I push my palm further and further
我看着我的手掌在玻璃边刃上	I watch my palm moving slowly
缓缓不停地向前进	along the sharp edge of the glass
狠着心，我把我的手掌一推到底	Steeling myself, I push my palm to the end
手掌的肉分开了	Flesh of my palm splits open
白色的肉和白色的骨头	white flesh and white bone
纯洁开始展开	Purity is hereby laid open

(tr. by Hai An & Cassandra Atherton)

各人

你和我各人各拿各人的杯子

我们各人各喝各的茶

我们微笑相互

点头很高雅

我们很卫生

各人说各人的事情

各人数各人的手指

各人发表意见

各人带走意见

最后，我们各人走各人的路

在门口我们握手

各人看着各人的眼睛

下楼梯的时候

如果你先走

我向你挥手

Each to Each

You and I each hold our own cups

We each drink our own tea

We smile at each other

And nod with elegance

We are quite hygienic

Each person speaks of his own affairs

Each person counts on his own fingers

Each person expresses an opinion

Each person comes away with an opinion

And finally they go their own way

In the doorway we shake hands

Each looking at the other's eyes

At the head of the stairs

If you are going first

I wave to you

说再来	Say *come again*
如果我先走	If I am going first
你也挥手	You wave at me
说慢走	Say *don't hurry*
然后我们各人各披各人的雨衣	And we each pull on our own parkas
如果下雨	If rain is falling
我们各自逃走	We run off in our own directions

(tr. by Denis Mair)

余刚　Yu Gang

余刚（1957–），诗人，现居杭州。出版过诗集《为生活写生》等。
Yu Gang, Chinese poet, born in 1957 at Hangzhou, is the author of several poetry books including *Sketching for Life*.

故人的问候　　　　　Greetings from an Old Friend

来自故人的问候，仿佛在江的对岸
那时，我们寻访青春的手记
全然不在心的内部
对史官的无知，导致梅花和竹子
还有松树，成为遥远的到达信号
并不知皮和毛的哲理
王朝和王朝更迭的前记
以及，时势的不明和群情激愤
有一个灰暗的分野

Greetings from an old friend, as if on the other side of the river
At that time, we searched for the recorded experiences of our
　youth
Completely from the heart
The ignorance of historians led to plum blossoms and bamboo
And pine trees, be a distant arrival signal
Notto know the philosophy of skin and hair
The foreword on dynastic change
The uncertain trend and public anger of the times

就在周边，以一种看得见的正直

逐步离开这里的空气

走向方岩和括苍山脉

听到了政治和气候的脉动

是怎样一种召唤，造就一个人

今日在大院的偶遇，是偶然又不是偶然

朴实依然，记忆依然

历练却是大相径庭

是什么在召唤，是什么从心底里升起

完成的似没有完成

无意中的却真正地写上一笔

(2013)

There appeared a gloomy divergence

Just nearby, a kind of visible integrity

Step by step, it came out of the air

Moved toward Fangyan and Kuocang Mountains

And heard the pulse of politics and climate change

What kind of a call to make a person

Is it accidental or not, to encounter this in the compound today?

Still simple in memory

Experience is entirely different

What is calling, what is rising from the bottom of my heart

Seemingly completed or not

It is unwittingly written out as a real stroke

(2013)

温柔

在面若桃花的特定时刻

你被一种桃花酒惊住了,直往后退

你又被一种烈性的空气所击中

手中举着的烟卷剧烈倒下

一种饱经沧桑的温柔,随即被自己烫伤

那不是烫伤,只是一种久未相见的朋友的惊喜

一种与世隔绝的惊讶

相信在这一刻,月亮愿意将自己擦拭一番

花儿愿意再次徐徐开放

只为了那不曾有或不需要有的回忆

人生何必回忆,见面就是自然的熟悉

可以称之为惊为天人吗,不说也罢

一个侧面的剪影使人想起俄罗斯人

Gentleness

At a specific time, in the face of peach blossoms

You were frightened by peach wine, and backed away

You were hit by strong air

The cigarette you held in your hand, fell violently

Your kind of gentleness has been scalded by the vicissitudes of life

Not only a scald, it's surprising for friends who have not seen you for a long time

A kind of surprise that's in incomplete isolation

I believed that at this moment, the moon was willing to wipe itself

Flowers were willing to come into bloom once again

Just for the memories of things that never existed, or aren't needed

What do you remember of life when meeting is a natural familiarity?

是哪一个呢，是最受苦受难还是较为受苦的
　　那个

无须分辨，只要不去注视鱼尾纹就好
只要记起岁月不再是血腥就好
花朵从不会寂寞开放，那些小城的人们
总会带来真诚，他们诚实的镜头
不会像水手在巴黎，但会像满脸皱纹的朴实
　　父亲

我忽然明白，莲花的地界，为何少见莲花
那是因为心不沉静，秋夜的烦躁不亚于夏夜
尽管我们已经没有烦躁，对于世界的荒唐事
不再感慨，因为，灞桥的树枝总归要折去
再远的花朵总得要有人欣赏

所有人都那么热烈，我却注意到有一个人落寞

Could we take her for a fairy, not to say the least ?
A lateral silhouette reminded me of the Russians
Which one, the one who suffered the most or
　　suffered the more ?

No need to distinguish, just do not stare at the
　　crows' feet
Just remember that the years were no longer bloody
Flowers never bloom lonely, people in small towns
Were always sincere, and appeared in honest shots
Not like a sailor in Paris, but like a plain, wrinkled
　　father

I suddenly understood why lotus flowers were rare
　　on their own land
Because our hearts were not quiet, autumn night was
　　less irritable than summer night
Although we were no longer irritable, no longer
　　deeply moved
By the absurd world, because the branches at *Baqiao*

也许天生就是沉静

不是自来熟的那种，有点像孤山的梅花

镇守长夜的梅花

与一颗暗淡的星有着天壤之别

没有别的，窗外一直散发

某种淡淡的气息

(2016)

eventually snapped

Flowers should be appreciated, no matter how far away

Everyone was so enthusiastic, but I noticed someone who
    was lonely

Maybe quiet by nature

Not like self-ripening, but a bit like plum blossom sat *Gushan*

Plum blossoms stood up for an eternal night

So different from a dim star

Nothing else, but outside the window the air

Kept giving off some faint breath

(2016)(tr. by Hai An & Cassandra Atherton)

王自亮 Wang Ziliang

王自亮(1958–)，诗人、作家，浙江台州人，现居杭州，浙江工商大学教授。出版诗集《将骰子掷向大海》《冈仁波齐》等。

Wang Ziliang, Chinese poet, writer, born in Taizhou, Zhejiang Province, currently serves as the professor at Zhejiang Industrial and Commercial University at Hangzhou. He is the author of several poetry books, including *Throwing Dices into the Sea* and *Mt. Kailash*.

握手

两只手伸出之前，各自在心里已把对方握过一
   遍了
手心尚未出血，玫瑰绽开，花园藏剑
也许，这只手是陆虎，另一只是捷豹
它们总是要碰到的：瞪眼，刨地，悻然离开
握，还是不握？"一行到此水西流"
这不是什么常识，也非准则
神迹出现是需要前提的：骤雨、道路与心
旷野诞生于仇人握手之际

Hand-Shaking

Both hands had been held in their hearts before reaching out
Palms not bleeding yet, roses in bloom, swords hidden in the
   garden
Maybe one hand is a Land Rover and the other is a Jaguar
They always come across: to glare, to plough the field and to
   leave resentfully
To shake hands, or not to? "A stream flows to the

别指望两手相握就一切妥帖

另一个信条是，不想握的手就再也不去握了

除非你是政客非得抓住那双伪造的手

听好多人说起（但记不得是谁）——

温软的手藏有杀气，多肉的手精神贫困

那就握住穷人的手吧，或者先知的手

正如水滴握住海洋，词握住语言，想象握住现实

west
   once Yi Xing reached here"

It is not common sense, nor a criterion

Miracles need premises: showers, roads, and inner hearts

The moors appear as the enemy shakes hands

Don't count on everything being done properly, once they
   shake hands

Another creed: never shake hands once more, if you don't
   want to

Unless you're a politician, you have to grab that fake hand

Many people mentioned (but I fail to remember who it
   was)—

Warm soft hands possess a killing power, but fleshy hands are
   poverty-stricken in spirit

Then hold the hands of the poor, or those of the prophet

Just as water drops grasp an ocean, words hold a language,
   magination gripps reality

(tr. by Hai An & Cassandra Atherton)

钟表店

许多钟表在沉睡。没有人能够
指出一次滴答所耗费的帝国银两：
流动的运河，无止境的游戏。
也没有人记载，行围狩猎时
夕阳的一片金黄色中，无数枝
穿透天空的箭簇，如何带着
时间的血迹，返回珐琅的钟面。

在钟表馆，没有人会去校准
难以叙述的"此刻"，以免碰坏
无数个特别的过去。唯一的心情
是制止那个著名的伦敦钟表匠，
与帝王合谋，砍下志士的头颅。
不再怀念在山冈上徘徊的起义者，
也没有人在宫殿的一角注意到，
那些形形色色的钟怎样走时报点：

The Clock Shop

The clocks are soundly asleep. No one can tell
how much imperial silver is spent in a tick-tock:
It's a running canal, an endless game.
Nor did anyone record how the hunting arrows.
pierced the sky in the golden sunset
tainted with blood of time,
and turned back to rest on the clock dial.

At the clock shop, no one would bother
to calibrate this indescribable "present" to avoid
breaking those special moments. The only thing in their mind
was to stop that notorious London clockmaker
who conspired with the king to behead the martyrs.
No one would remember the rebels hovering on the mountain
    ridges,
Nor would anyone notice how clocks of all kinds and sizes
chimed around the corner of the palace:
opening a door, playing music or a puppet show, or other
    tricks.

开门、奏乐和禽戏，或更多的用途。
没有谁留心究竟是发条，还是
惊奇的坠砣，带动齿轮毕生劳作。

在钟表馆，没有多少人想知晓
一个雨天的闲谈中所割让的疆土，
了解大臣与时钟，献媚的技艺。
从朝廷的传言，到斩首的邀请，
情形复杂得像座钟无与伦比的内部。
而人心的法则却像指针那样简洁，
有时成一个夹角，有时如一支响箭。

(2004)

Nobody cares whether it's the spring or the amazing weight
that drives the gears to lifelong labour.

At the clock shop, nobody wants to know
the territorial concessions one could make
in a casual talk, in a raining day.
To understand the ministers and clocks, the same art of
　ingratiation.
From court rumors to an invitation to a beheading,
The situation is as complex as the marvelous interior of a
　mantle clock.
The law of people's will, however, is as simple as the
　pointer,
Sometimes folded at an angle,
sometimes straight as an arrow,

(2004) (tr. by Ajiu cassandra Atherton)

陈先发 Chen Xianfa

陈先发（1967-），诗人，安徽桐城人。著有诗集《春天的死亡之书》《前世》《写碑之心》《养鹤问题》《裂隙与巨眼》等。

Chen Xianfa, Chinese poet, born in Tongcheng, Anhui Province, has published several anthologies of poetry, including *Death in Springtime, A Past Life, Engraved Monument of the Heart, On Raising Cranes,* and *Fissures* and *Giant Eyes*.

孤岛的蔚蓝

卡尔维诺说，重负之下人们
会奋不顾身扑向某种轻

成为碎片。在把自己撕成更小
碎片的快慰中认识自我

我们的力量只够在一块
碎片上固定自己

Lonely Island Sapphire

According to Italo Calvino, people weighed down
   by heavy loads
will ignore danger just to go for lightness

becoming fragments. And while they're jubilantly
   ripping themselves into tinier
bits they're getting to know themselves.

We have just enough strength to

折枝。写作。频繁做梦——
围绕不幸构成短暂的暖流

感觉自己在孤岛上。
岛的四周是

很深的拒绝或很深的厌倦
才能形成的那种蔚蓝

(2017)

fix ourselves on these bits

snapping a twig. Writing. Frequently dreaming—
around misfortune to gather tentative temperate
   tidal motion

I feel myself lonely upon islands
encircled by

a sapphire-colored-color shaped by
deep dejection, deeper boredom

(2017)

秋兴九章之五

每时每刻。镜中那个我完好
无损。只是退得远远的——

人终须勘破假我之境
譬如夜半窗前听雨

总觉得万千雨滴中，有那一滴
在分开众水，独自游向湖心亭

汹涌而去的人流中，有
那么一张脸在逆风回头

人终须埋掉这些
生动的假我。走得远远的

当灰烬重新成为玫瑰

Nine Poems on Inspirations of Autumn (5)

Each instant. In mirrors I'm an intact

undamaged-whole-piece. But, retreating, away, farther-
    away—

Persons must, at the end of the day, finally break away from
    "fake" self-identity
When listening to rain sounds at mine night window

I'm feeling that, among 10s of 1000s of raindrops, there's that
    one drop
that leaves all others, and goes swimming lone to the lake
    centre pavilion

Amid crowd roaring there's

more often than not that one Face turning round, round &

还有几双眼睛认得?

秋风中，那么深刻的

隐身衣和隐形人……

(2016)

round against the wind

Persons have to, when it comes down to it, bury these

yes very vivid but really "fake" self-identities.

Walk away, away farther

When ash turns rose again

how few, few, the pairs of eyes that recognize ?

In autumn wind, there are extremely profound

invisible cloaks, invisible persons···

(2016) (tr. by a.j. carruthers)

雷武铃 Lei Wuling

雷武铃(1968-),诗人、文学批评家,出生于湖南,现为河北大学文学院教授。出版诗集《赞颂》,主编诗刊《相遇》。
Lei Wuling, poet and literary critic, born in Hunan in 1968, is a professor at the School of Arts at Hebei University and the editor-in-chief of colleagues poetry magazine, *"Encounter"*, publishing a collection of poems, *Praise*.

冬天的树

1

从温暖,明亮,深邃的书中出来

正是最迷乱的时刻:公共汽车轰鸣

车灯,路灯,橱窗灯交织的浮光与暗影里

漂浮着表情模糊,行色慌忙的人。

那么多,那么乱,又那么不真实的虚影

我们抬头,看见前面

两道壁立的黑色悬崖之间

Trees in Winter

1

Emerging from warm, illuminating books

just at the most confusing moment: buses roaring

headlights, streetlights, window lights, interwoven with
   floating light and shadow

accompanied by a vague, hasty person

So much. So chaotic. And such an unreal virtual shadow.

We looked up and saw a crimson sunset, low in the dark-
   blue sky

between two black cliffs in front of us.

幽蓝的天空低处一道暗红色晚霞
黑色树枝映满天空,那么清晰,一动不动
超然于混乱和寒冷之上。

2

我们说起冬天的树。
那么安静,即使大风呼啸,也只是轻轻晃动的树。
它们的美难以言传:大块密闭的色团
落成天幕上镂空的线条画,——它活生生的
能透出呼吸。车过公园,能看见绵延的树丛
和后面的天空。——它们阴晴天的表情不同:
树干焦黑,爪状的枝梢蜷缩高空的,是槐树。
树皮灰白,粗枝和银杏树一样高举的是白杨。
而榆树和柳树的枝条众多,轻柔地向下垂顾。
而核桃树枝粗短如手指,整个冬天都在沉睡。

Black branches filled the sky, clear and motionless
above the chaos and cold.

2

We talked about the winter trees.
Trees, so quiet, they only shook gently, even if the wind
   whistled.
Their indescribable beauty: a large, closed mass of color
created a hollowed-out skyline—it breathed.
From the car, you could see bushes stretching across the
   park
with sky behind them—their appearance was different
   on sunny or cloudy days:
the locust tree with black trunks, claw-shaped branches
   curling up high above;
the poplar tree with grey bark, the thick branches as
   high as the ginkgo tree.
The elm and willow branches were numerous, gently
   hanging down
Walnut branches were as short as fingers, sleeping all
   winter.

3

我们相信有这样一个地方:
那里山峦绵延,从来无人到达
几百万、上千万亩的树林在中午的太阳下
落光了叶子。那些安静的山谷
和山坡上,我们走动
枯枝落叶就响起干燥的声响,腾起灰尘。
我们停下,纯净无边的阳光
就从头顶灌注,消融我们的眼睛。
我们做好了准备。但终于没有去成。
而雪肯定下到了那里,——那些雪中的树。

(2003)

3

We believed there was a place:
where mountains stretched, that no one ever reached.
Millions of acres of trees shed leaves in the midday sun.
On those quiet valleys and hillsides, we walked around.
The withered branches and fallen leaves echoed with a
  dry and dusty sound.
We stopped and the pure and boundless sun
Poured into our skulls and melted our eyes.
We are prepared. Yet we have never been.
And the snow must have fallen there—those trees in the
  snow.

(2003)

白云（二）

耀眼的湛蓝色光芒在河谷上空流溢。

一朵唯一的白云，色泽纯净、曲线柔和，悬浮在北边合围的岭头后面、那座横亘半空的青色大山之前。

它在空中近乎不动。它的大片投影像黑色丝绸，颤抖着从明亮的山体斜掠而下。

有一阵，消逝不见了。然后，出现在前面的岭头从那里飘下，顺着河谷的东侧向南滑行。

现在，它高出了青色山体的背景，它的雪白被天空的湛蓝映射，亮得几乎透明。

少年的我被惊喜充盈，它真的如我所愿向我飘来。

我惊异远处过来的云影，那超然的神秘：

它不择道路，不避高低，被非凡的力量推动无视稻田、山坡、河岸、田埂的差别，径自向前。

巨轮般压倒一切又轻盈如蝴蝶，梦一样

White Clouds (II)

The bright blue rays flowed over the valley.

A single white cloud, was suspended in the north behind the ridge of the dark blue mountains; its soft curves on the skyline.

It was almost stationary in the air. Its large form like black silk, slid down from the bright mountain.

For a while, it disappeared. Then floated down from the front ridge and glided south along the east side of the valley.

Then it was above the background of the blue mountain,the azure blue sky reflected in its snow white transparency.

As teenage, I was filled with surprises,

really floating to me as I was,amazed by the transcendental mystery of the distant cloud:

it chose no path, avoided no height, but was pushed by extraordinary forces

to ignore the differences between paddy fields, hills,banks, and ridges.

染暗白亮的阳光像风吹皱粼粼波面。

它向我飞近，速度越来越快

凉意夹着大片草叶细密的窸窣声

风一样，从离我最近的河面、稻田，过去了。

它的背影，飘上南边起伏的、白光覆照的山头。

在更南边白炽的空中，那形状已变的云，停留了一阵，

也消散了。天空只剩下唯一的湛蓝。

河谷张开着，容接垂直降落的阳光。

河边稻田璀璨的青黄，山腰油茶树坚硬油亮的深绿，

山顶松树闪耀的银光，渐次由低到高；点缀在

山间的红壤耕地，红薯叶、玉米叶摇动的绿色

由近及远，绵延向远处柔和的草山。

这些不规则的坡面、色块、光斑，从不同的高

It overwhelmed everything as a giant wheel, yet was light as a butterfly

and transformed white sunlight to darkness as if in a dream; the wind ruffling its sparkling face.

It flew closer to me, gaining pace,

passing through the nearest river and paddy field like a cold wind

with a thick rustle of grass and leaves

Its back floated south of the undulating, white-covered mountain,

Farther south, in the incandescent sky farther, the changing cloud stayed for a while

and then dissipated. There was only blue left in the sky.

The valley opened, allowing the sun to fall vertically.

The rice field was emerald green, it was yellow by the river, and oil-tea camellia was dark green on the hillside.

On top of the mountain, the silver light reflected on the pine tree changed from bright to muted;

the cultivated land of red soil in the mountains, was

低和远近

把它们变幻的反光折射向河谷，汇成浮动的斑斓。

我坐在西边山沿松树的习习荫凉下，能看到

炽烈光芒中整条河水的流向。

从北边合围的山底出来，两道平行的绿色河岸

在稻田间直行。不见河水，一道木桥横跨其上。

第二个转弯处，一堆白雪在那里闪耀——

是河水从堰坝落下。寂静的空气震颤

落水的轰鸣声飘忽而悠远，分辨不出来处。

另一处河湾，河水在鹅卵石浅滩上流溅波光。

对面山脚北去的石板路上，打伞的行人就要折

   向木桥了

山坳上，庄稼中露出的半个戴草帽的身影，始

   终未动。

风吹草木，光的波浪起伏，从山坡、稻田一排

dotted with green sweet potato leaf and corn leaves

shook in the breeze,

stretching to the distant soft grass hills

These irregular slopes, patches, and spots refracted their varying reflections to the valley

from different heights and distances, converging into floating beauty,

Sitting in the shade of the pine trees on the west side of the mountain,

I could see the flow of the whole river in the blazing light.

From the bottom of the north side of the hill, two parallel green riverbanks

ran straight between rice fields. A wooden bridge straddled the river without water.

At the second turn, a pile of snow flashed—

a river fell from the weir dam. The silent air trembled.

Fallen water was roaring, remote and dimly discernible.

排传来。

热烈的空气、蝉声，大黑蚂蚁爬上我脸。

噢，两朵新的白云，扁平如梭，一前一后，连绵着

从北边高山的后面睡梦般飘出。

一朵向东，沉入山后。一朵飘到了河谷上空。

那雪白的云朵悠然如万古，浮游于碧蓝光芒的无限。

(2005)

On the other river bend, the river splashed on the cobblestone shoal.

On the slate road north cross the foot of the hill, the pedestrian was holding up umbrellas ready to return to the wooden bridge,

And among the hills, a figure bared half a straw hat and the crops never moved

The wind blew the trees, the waves of light rose and fell from the hillside and the rice paddies.

In the warm air, cicadas made a cacophony as a big black ant climbed up my face.

Oh, two new white clouds, flattened as a shuttle, the one behind the other,

blew out behind the north mountain.

One went east, sinking behind the mountain. One floated over the valley.

The snow-white clouds are everlasting, floating in the boundless blue light.

(2005) (tr. by Hai An & Cassandra Atherton)

海男　Hai Nan

海男（1962-），诗人、小说家，云南永胜人。第六届鲁迅文学奖得主，现居昆明，著有诗集《虚构的玫瑰》等。
Hai Nan, Chin poetess and novelist, was born in 1962 at Yongsheng, Yunnan Province. As the winner of the sixth *Lu Xun Literature Prize*, currently living at Kunming. She is the author of many books including poetry book, *Fictional Rose*.

简约

简约，是呼吸中起伏的麦粒

颗粒饱满，就这样我已知足

鞋子是要旧的，迈向那凹陷处

祖国的版图是需要铁匠的

远隔山川，手抚摸处是棉花更多的是蛛丝马迹

更多的是寒冷的峡谷区域

那一只只迷失方向的精灵

用哪一种指南针寻找到你小木屋的炭火

简约，就像旧书架上一只蝴蝶的标本

Simplicity

Simplicity is the rippling grain of breath

Plump-eared grain, and so I am content that

Shoes should be worn-out, towards the caved ground

The territory of our country needs a blacksmith

Far away from the mountains, the touch of a hand is cotton, more of a clue

More of a cold canyon area

What kind of compass is used by the elves who got lost

Finding the charcoal fire in your cabin

没有人要你的金矿,札记,戒指
没有人要你的宝典,诗歌,色空
但有人想听见你劈柴的声音,斧头下的碎屑
还有人想弯下腰,为你洗一次头发
还有人热爱你的指甲。在我的开始
是我的结束,这是诗人艾略特的诗句
而我的诗句,埋在坛子里
理所当然,它们应该埋在坛子里
成为化石,就像云南古老的游牧民族
面对闪电惊悚,用陶器掘起一座山坡,埋藏下
　　不说话的前世咒语

Simplicity is like a specimen of a butterfly on an old
　　shelf
No one wants your gold mine, reading notes or
　　finger ring
No one wants your valuable book, poems or
　　nonexistent form
But someone wants to hear you chopping wood, the
　　crumbs under an axe
Someone else wants to bend down, to wash your
　　hair once
Someone else loves your nail. In my beginning is my
　　end
That is the line written by T.S. Eliot
And my verse, buried in the jar
Of course, should be buried in the jar
As a fossil, like an ancient nomad of Yunnan
In the face of lightning horror, pottery dug up on a
　　hillside is the buried unspoken mantra of the past

西南之隅，无限美好

我喜欢早晨，甚于夜晚

一切妖魔鬼怪将退下。早晨的空茫

干干净净，比如睡眼在清泉中洗过

早晨，脚步轻盈，每每推窗

全世界都是新人新语。我喜欢早晨

甚于喜欢夜晚，当黑暗退下

我就可以区别梦书，在哪一页中蝉是欢鸣的

白鹤已直上云端，我喜欢早晨

甚于喜欢在黑夜中的迷途

早茶已煮好，败北之路已修好独木桥

西南之隅，无限美好

古朴的面孔，河谷和丘陵比肩接邻

我成为它其中的一种符号

就像蛇已经蜕过皮，心魔度过了天荒

我喜欢早晨，甚于喜欢长夜之烛

当曙光垂临，我看见的葵花已逝

The Southwest Corner is of Infinite Beauty

I prefer the morning to the night

All demons will retreat. The morning is empty

Clean and fresh, as sleeping eyes washed in a clear spring

In the morning, graceful on my footstep, whenever I open the window

The world is full of newlyweds. I prefer the morning

To the night, when the darkness recedes

I can distinguish the dream book, in which pages sing as cicadas

The crane gone up to the clouds, I prefer the morning

To the night, lost in the dark

I have boiled up water for a morning tea, a single-log bridge on the road repaired by the builder

The southwest corner is of infinite beauty

A quaint appearance, valleys and hills side by side

我改变不了初衷和自然之宿

因此，我拍击翅膀，这一刻

我不再是煎熬。我喜欢早晨

是因为可以逢着一束天光

由此可见，我的喜悦正在冉冉上升

I become one of its symbols

As a snake has sloughed its skin and the demon has gone through the wilderness.

I prefer the morning to the candle of eternal night

As the dawn falls, the sunflower I see is gone

I can't change my original intention and natural night.

So, I flap my wings, at this moment

I am no longer tormented. I prefer the morning

Because I can meet a ray of daylight

From now on, my joy is rising slowly.

(tr. by Hai An & Cassandra Atherton)

潘洗尘　Pan Xichen

潘洗尘（1964–），诗人，黑龙江人，2009年创办天问诗歌艺术节。出版诗集《我们看海去》《这是我一直爱着的黑夜》等。
Pan Xichen, Chinese poet born in 1964 in Heilongjiang Province, created the *Tianwen* Poetry and Arts Festival in 2009. He is the author of several poetry books including *We Go for the Sea, It is the Night I've been in Love with*.

残忍的秋天

从初秋到深秋

我发现把一个秋天完整地看完

是很残忍的

就说窗前的这片稻田吧

露珠一天比一天少了

稻穗一天比一天黄了

当所有人都将为果实欢呼的时候

我却从这饱满的成熟中

The Cruel Autumn

From early autumn to late autumn

I find it cruel

To have to sit through the whole autumn

Just say the rice fields are at the window

There are fewer and fewer dewdrops day after day

The rice ears are more and more yellow

As everyone cheers for the fruit

I have found death

From full maturity

看到了死亡

仅以其中的一棵稻穗为例
虽然每一粒果实还可以作为种子
在明年发芽
但今年的这棵稻穗
却是以死亡为代价
才完成最后的成熟
也最终以成熟的方式
走向了死亡

你说秋天是走向成熟的季节
我说秋天是等待死亡的过程

Only take one rice ear as an example
Though each fruit can germinate
As a seed next year
The rice ear of this year
Never accomplishes its final maturity
Until it risks death
And eventually heads for death
In a mature way

You say autumn is a season for maturity
I say autumn is a process waiting for death

盐碱地

在北方松嫩平原的腹部
大片大片的盐碱地
千百年来没生长过一季庄稼
连成片的艾草也没有
春天过后一望无际的盐碱地
与生命有关的
只有散落的野花
和零星的羊只
但与那些肥田沃土相比
我更爱这平原里的荒漠
它们亘古不变默默地生死
就像祖国多余的部分

Saline–alkali Land

In the central Songnen Plain of the North
There is a large area of saline-alkali land
For thousands of years it has never grown a season
   of crops
Not even a large area of wormwoods
On the boundless saline-alkali land after spring
There scatters several wild flowers
And sporadic sheep
Related to life
But compared to the fertile soil
I love the wildness more in the plain
They live and die eternally in silence
As an extra part of our country

(tr. by Hai An & Cassandra Atherton)

伊沙　Yi Sha

伊沙（1966–），诗人，生于四川成都，现执教于西安外国语大学。出版诗集《饿死诗人》《野种之歌》《我终于理解了你的拒绝》《伊沙诗选》等。

Yi Sha, Chinese poet born in 1966 at Chengdu, Sichuan Province, currently teaches at Xi'an International Studies University. He is the author of several poetry books including *Starve the Poets, Song of the Bastard, I Finally Understand Why You Reject Me* and *Selected Poems by Yi Sha*.

车过黄河　　　　　　　　Crossing the Yellow River

列车正经过黄河

我正在厕所小便

我深知这不该

我　应该坐在窗前

或站在车门旁边

左手叉腰

右手作眉檐

眺望　像个伟人

至少像个诗人

As the train was passing over the Yellow River

I was in the toilet having a piss

Oh, I knew I was being remiss

I should have been sitting at one of the windows

or standing by a door of the carriage

left hand on my hip

shielding my eyes with my right hand

gazing out like some Great Man

or like a poet, at the very least

recalling some anecdote connected with this river

or some episode from its history

想点河上的事情

或历史的陈账

那时人们都在眺望

我在厕所里

时间很长

现在这时间属于我

我等了一天一夜

只一泡尿工夫

黄河已经流远

Just then, everyone was gazing out the window

while I was in the toilet

for what seemed like ages

for my time had come

I had waited 24 hours for this

but in the time it took to have a piss

I'd left the Yellow River a long way behind me

(tr. by Simon Patton & Tao Naikan)

结结巴巴

结结巴巴我的嘴
二二二等残废
咬不住我狂狂狂奔的思维
还有我的腿

你们四处流流流淌的口水
散着霉味
我我我的肺
多么劳累

我要突突突围
你们莫莫莫名其妙的节奏
急待突围

我我我的
我的机枪点点点射般的语言

Stutter

my stu-stu-stuttering mouth
sec-sec-second degree handicap
can't bite my ra-ra-racing thoughts
or into my thighs

your spu-spu-sputtering spit
stinks of fun-fun-fungus
how weary
my-my-my lungs

i need to esc-esc-escape
your puz-puz-puzzling rhythm
has trapped me too long

mm-mm-my words
shoo-shoo-shoot
happily as a ma-machinegun

my stu-stu-stuttering life

充满快慰

结结巴巴我的命

我的命里没没没有鬼

你们瞧瞧瞧我

一脸无所谓

has nn-nn-no ghost

take a look at my face

covered with in-in-indifference

(Tr. by Wang Ping & Alex Lemon)

马非 Ma Fei

马非（1971–），诗人，生于辽宁，现居青海。出版诗集《宝贝》等7部。
Ma Fei, Chinese poet, born in 1971 in Liaoning, currently lives in Qinghai. He is the author of seven poetry collections including *Baby*.

一把铁锹 / Shovel

雪后中午

在麒麟湾公园

偏僻的一角

一小片树林之间

我看见一把铁锹

支在其中一棵树上

还有两行脚印

从我站立的小径

迤逦到那里

---

noon after snow

Kirin Bay Park

there where there's a far corner

in this patch of wood

a shovel I see

stuck up a tree

two print-foot-trails

snake along

here from the path where I stand

sunbeam

这时一束阳光
从枝杈处倾泻而下
铁锹猛然一颤
仿佛活了
闪闪发光
逼人眯眼
白雪也顿失其白
惊起两只乌鸦
和一伙麻雀
扑棱棱四散开去

it streams down through those branches there
suddenly, the shovel quivers
it's as if it's having a *soul*
gleams
dazzled light
snow forsaken by íts whiteness
the two crows and with them a flock of sparrows
the lot of them frightened
flee with cláttʼring wing

伟大的战争

我所知道的

堪称伟大的战争

不是特洛伊战争

不是苏联的卫国战争

不是十四年抗战

而是发生在不久前

中印边境摩擦引发的

以小孩子过家家的方式

互掷石块摔上几跤之后

就不了了之的战争

双方的伤亡为零

Great War

the war one may refer to as "Great"

according to my knowledge, as far as I know,

isn't the Trojan War

isn't the Great Patriotic War of the Union of Soviet
    Socialist Republics,

nor is it the Eight-Year Anti-Japanese War in this,
    my country,

however the one triggered

by some certain and quite recent Sino-Indian

cross-border friction or tension

might be said to be comparable to a children's game

where they, or both, end up with nothing

after a bout of wrestling and about of tickling

no casualties

(tr. by a.j. carruthers & Cui Yuwei)

王敖 Wang Ao

王敖(1976-)，诗人，美国威斯里安大学副教授，耶鲁大学博士。曾获安高诗歌奖和《人民文学》新人奖。译有史蒂文斯、克兰、奥登、希尼等人作品。

Wang Ao, poet and translator, an associate professor of Chinese literature at the Wesleyan University, received his PhD. from the Yale University. He has been the recipient of prizes such as the Anne Kao Poetry Prize and the New Poet Prize from *People's Literature*. He has translated the work of poets such as Wallace Stevens, Hart Crane, W.H. Auden, and Seamus Heaney into Chinese.

冬夜站在加油站我怕什么

Standing at the Gas Station on a Winter's Night, What Am I Afraid Of

习惯了长途奔袭的司机，我看着
加油站周围的鸽子，它们等待着快餐店出来的
　人不慎落下薯条

几个面目不清的人，在寒风中等着零活，他们
　加鸽子
让麦当劳大叔有点像基督，我怕这些吗

A driver used to long-haul raids, I watch
pigeons by the gas station, waiting for fries dropped people
　coming out of the fast food joint

a few people with obscured faces wait in the cold wind for
　odd jobs, they and the pigeons
make Ronald McDonald sort of look like Jesus—is that
　what I'm afraid of

我并不怕这些，虽然我是个中国人，王小波的
　　弟弟王晨光
就是在公路旁遇袭，但我告诉你我练过，你觉
　　得没用

但我已习惯了，在圣路意斯也好，在芝加哥郊
　　区的汽车旅馆也好
从内心深处做到了，接近浑不吝的镇定，因为
　　在光线不好的情况下

长头发、脚步急促、眼神略疯狂的我，曾被同
　　学误认暴徒，当然我不是
也因此不瞎担心什么，真正让我害怕的

哪个更可能轮到我身上，具体的就不多说了，
　　但这种感觉追逐着我
让我的影子，从猎犬变成野马，变成更可怕的
　　猎食动物，如果我走在家乡的马路上

no, I'm not afraid of that, although I'm Chinese—Wang
　　Xiaobo's little brother Wang Chenguang
was attacked on the street, but let me tell you I've been in
　　fights, you think it doesn't matter

but I'm used to it, in Saint Louis or a motel on the outskirts
　　of Chicago
I've achieved it deep within myself, an unflappable cool,
　　since
　　in a dimly-lit situation

with my long hair and quick steps and slightly crazy eyes, a
　　classmate once took me for a thug
of course I'm not but that doesn't make me worry—what
　　really makes me afraid

which is more likely to affect me, there's no need to say, but
　　the feeling follows me
turning my shadow from a hunting dog into a wild horse i
　　into an even more terrifying animal at hunt, and so if I
　　were

我会因此充满攻击性,敢惹我的人还没有出生,
　爆炸发生时
气浪扭曲了街道,难道不更适合我去走一圈吗,
　你以为我真的害怕吗

童年的友伴,在化工厂上班的向东哥,已经因
　癌症去世
隔壁的邻居,被人打傻了,在疯人院不会再有
　人给他买烟

我感到的恐惧,并不是因为命运无情而果断,
　佛经已经解释了
我梦中的大山大海就在身后,仿佛都是预言,
　只有规模浩大,不清楚具体何指

我害怕那种赤脚的不怕穿鞋的式的心态,就是
　在这里出了问题

walking down the street in my hometown
I'd be aggressive, those who'd dare bother me haven't even
　been born, and the blast
distorted the street, and that might be even better for me to
　walk down, and did you think I'm actually afraid

my childhood friend Xiangdong who worked in a chemical
　plant, already dead from cancer
my next door neighbor, beaten to brain damage and stuck in
　a madhouse where no one will ever buy him cigarettes
　again

the dread I feel isn't because fate is ruthless and decisive, the
　sutras have explained that
in my dreams the mountains and oceans are behind me, as
　though it's a prophecy, but the scope is so big the details
　are unclear

i fear the mentality of my feet not being afraid to wear shoes,
　that's where the problem lies.

想做英雄更接近妄想,即使你在国外,也怀疑
　　如果什么发生了
也许是同胞第一个下手,我怕这种心态,我也
　　反感那种浑不吝

翻扣在自己的睡眠中,听到猛禽的羽翅划着风
　　声就像切纸
这种情况下,恐惧跟是否勇敢完全无关,它关
　　乎因果链的简单模型背后

千万个踩灭希望的脚步,在史诗开始前的十年,
　　已经有无数人无声地倒下

这个问题根本不存在,甲虫在水下能闭气跑
　　四十分钟,因此适应了
对它们非常不友好的地球,从石油形成的年代
　　算起就赢了,它们为自己的

trying to be a hero is just wishful thinking, and even if you're
　　abroad, you suspect that if something happens
it will be set off by your countrymen—I fear this attitude, I
　　hate this kind of unflappable cool

of dread in my sleep, hearing the wings of birds of prey
　　flapping like the sound of cut paper
at such moments, perhaps fear is unrelated to bravery, it has
　　to do with millions of hope-crushing feet

stepping behind the simple mold of cause and effect, ten
　　years before epic poetry, countless people had already
　　silently collapsed

this really isn't a question, beetles can survive under water for
　　forty minutes, so they can adapt
to an unfriendly world, and in an age of oil they win, they feel
　　contented

with their lack of security, and of course I want to be like that
　　too, when my hometown explodes to look like its own

缺乏安全感而感到怡然，我当然也想那样，当　　　　reflection in a funhouse mirror
　　我的家乡被炸得像照进了哈哈镜

　　　　　　　　　　　　　　　　　　　　　　　　　　　　　　　　　　(2013)

　　　　　　　　　　　　　　(2013)

新年夜话

诗的城市,音乐的有轨电车行驶在
雪后树枝的地图上,有一朵椰子味的比喻,也
   是风的耳垂

在我们的谈话背后,还有降落伞盛开
混沌,深渊,漩涡,都是它开的关于乌贼的玩笑,
   什么

世界的地基就是无穷无尽的长蛇
盘着一只大海龟吗,你的深呼吸,临时造就了
   深海的好奇

起源的故事,总有类似的黑洞在唱歌,尽管浪
   漫却武断
一个就自残造天地,双方则缠绵到今天,让毕
   达哥拉斯都无法

New Year's Eve Talk

in the city of poetry, the musical tramcar glides
on the atlas of a snowy tree branch, there's a
   coconut-flavored metaphor, which is also the
   wind's earlobe

behind our talk, a parachute blooms open
chaos, abysses, whirlpools, they're all its jokes about
   cuttlefish, and what?

is the world's foundation a tireless serpent
coiled around a huge sea turtle? For a moment your
   breathing trains the sea's curiosity

all genesis stories have similar singing black holes,
   romantic but arbitrary
one side sacrificing itself to create heaven and earth,
   both still intertwined, so Pythagoras

can't predict when the snow will fall again, or which

准确预言雪何时再次飘起，我们谁先入睡，颤   of us will sleep first, trembling in a zithered
   动梦乡琴声的小地震   dream of earthquakes

(2013)   (2013)（tr. by Eleanor Goodman）

胡续东　Hu Xudong

胡续冬(1974–)，诗人，本名胡旭东，生于重庆，曾就读于北京大学中文系和西方语言文学系，获文学博士学位。后执教于北京大学外国语学院世界文学研究所。已出版诗集8部，亦从事诗歌翻译。

Hu Xudong, Chinese poet, critic, essayist and translator, born in 1974 in Chongqing, now lives in Beijing. M.A. in Comparative Literature and Ph.D. in Contemporary Chinese Literature from Peking University, he teaches at the same university. He published 8 books of poetry and some translations of poems.

一个拣鲨鱼牙齿的男人

一个拣鲨鱼牙齿的男人，

弓着腰、撅着已近中年的屁股，

在沙与海水之间搜寻。

换作在他的故乡、他的童年，

这个姿势更像是在把少年水稻

插进东亚泥土旺盛的生殖循环里。

但请相信我，此刻他的确是在

拣鲨鱼的牙齿，在佛罗里达的

萨拉索塔县，在一个

叫作玛纳索塔的狭长的小岛西侧

A Man Who Collects Sharks' Teeth

A man who collects sharks' teeth,
bends down, sticking up his soon-to-be middle-
　　aged ass,
searching between the sand and sea.
if this were his hometown, during his youth,
this posture would be more likely that of planting
　　young rice into the exuberant life cycle of East
　　Asian soil.
But please trust me, right now he really is
collection sharks' teeth, in Florida's
Sarasota County, on the west side

濒临墨西哥湾的海滩上。
像着了魔一般,他已经拣了
整整一个下午,虽然灼人的烈日
似要将他熔成一团白光,但
每拣得一颗牙齿,他就感觉身上
多了一条鲨鱼的元气。那些
乌黑、闪亮、带着不容置疑的
撕咬的迫切性的牙齿,是被海水
挽留下来的力量的颗粒,是
静止在细沙里的嗜血的加速度,
是大海深处巨大的残暴之美被潮汐
颠倒了过来,变成了小小一枚
美之残暴。他紧攥着这些
余威尚存的尖利的小东西,这些
没有皮肉的鲨鱼,想象着
在深海一样昏暗的中年生活里,
自己偶尔也能朝着迎面撞来的厄运
亮出成千上万颗鲨鱼的牙齿。

(2008)

of a long narrow island called Manasota Key
near the beaches of the Gulf of Mexico.
As though under a spell, he has already spent
an entire afternoon collecting, although the
    scorching sun
is about to melt him into a ball of white light, but
with every collected tooth, he feels his body
has gained the vitality of a shark. Those
jet-black, gleaming teeth that carry the unassailable
urgency of ripping and tearing, are little grains
of power retained by the ocean, are
bloodthirsty acceleration made motionless in fine
    sand,
are the great brutal beauty of the depths of the ocean,
reversed by the tides, becoming a small bit
of the beautiful brutality. He grasps these
sharp, still powerful little things, these
fleshless sharks' teeth, imagining
that in middle age, dark as the deep sea,
he might show these thousands upon thousands of
sharks' teeth to the misfortunes that collide with him
    head-on.

(2008) (Manasota Key, Florida)

白猫脱脱迷失

公元568年，一个粟特人
从库思老一世的萨珊王朝
来到室点密的西突厥，给一支
呼罗珊商队当向导。在
疲惫的伊犁河畔，他看见
一只白猫蹲伏于夜色中，
像一片怛逻斯的雪，四周是
干净的草地和友善的黑暗。
他看见白猫身上有好几个世界
在安静地旋转，箭镞、血光、
屠城的哭喊都消失在它
白色的漩涡中。几分钟之后，
他放弃了他的摩尼教信仰。
1439年之后，
在夜归的途中，我和妻子
也看见了一只白猫，约莫有

The White Cat Toqtamish

in 568 AD, a Sogdian
came to Istami's Western Turkic Khaganate
from Khosrau the First's Sassanids, to serve as a guide
to a caravan of traders from Khrurasan.
on the tired banks of the Ili River he saw
a white cat crouching in the color of night
like a patch of snow in Talas, surrounded
by clean meadows and friendly darkness.
he saw several worlds on the white cat's body
calmly swirling. Arrows, bloodshed,
cries from the slaughtered city all disappeared
in its white whirlpool. After a few moments,
he gave up on Manichaeism.
one thousand four hundred thirty-nine years later,
in the middle of the night, my wife and I
also see a white cat,
about three months old, small but dignified as he strolls
by the dried-up pool of the Weixiu Garden,
like the crown prince of the last dynasty, crossing

三个月大，小而有尊严地

在蔚秀园干涸的池塘边溜达，

像一个前朝的世子，穿过

灯影中的时空，回到故园

来巡视它模糊而高贵的记忆。

它不躲避我们的抚摸，但也

不屑于我们的喵喵学语，隔着

一片树叶、一朵花或是

一阵有礼貌的夜风，它兀自

嗅着好几个世界的气息。

它试图用流水一般的眼神

告诉我们什么，但最终它还是

像流水一样弃我们而去。

我们认定它去了公元1382年

的白帐汗国，我们管它叫

脱脱迷失，它要连夜赶过去

征服钦察汗、治理俄罗斯。

(2007)

time and space in the lamp's shadow, returning to the

old garden to survey his obscure but noble memories.

he doesn't avoid our touch, but

won't respond to our babbled cat-speak; separated

by a leaf, a flower,

the polite night breeze, he concentrates

on taking in the scents of many worlds.

he tries to use his liquid eyes

to tell us something, but in the end

he leaves us like flowing water.

we think he went to the White Horde

of 1382, what we call Toqtamish,

wanting to set out at night

to conquer the Golden Horde and rule over Russia.

(2007) (tr. by Eleanor Goodman & Wang Ao)

冷霜　Leng Shuang

冷霜（1973-），诗人，毕业于北京大学中文系，文学博士，现任教于中央民族大学。著有诗集《我们年龄的雾》，曾获刘丽安诗歌奖、首届"诗建设"新锐诗人奖等。

Leng Shuang, Chinese poet, was born in 1973, currently teaching at Minzu University of China after receiving his PhD degree from Peking University. He is the author of poetry collection *The Fog of our age* was published in and won a few poetry prize such as Liu Li'an prize for poetry and *Poetry Construction Prize* (2013).

我们年龄的雾 / The Fog of Our Age

它是怎么来的：这是一个谜。
并非无法解开，只是我宁愿
为自己保留少许神秘性。

如同一只蜗牛，顺着台阶，
贴着墙，我目力所及之处
都已留下它牛乳般的痕迹：

我有意忽略了它的重量，

How it got here is a puzzle.
That's not to say it's unsolvable, but I'd rather
keep a little mystery for myself.

Snail-like, up the steps,
against the wall; wherever I look
I see its milky trail:

I intentionally ignore its weight,

不过，这倒是因为我深知
它的力量。我已领略过多次。

同样，我也从不担心
能见度之类的问题：我注意到
在它腹中有一所漂浮的邮局。

就这样，一日三餐，夜间散步，
睡前读几页帕斯卡尔。
窗户开着。我感到了变化。

因此我一度最感兴趣的是
它的边缘究竟在哪里，
结果总是使我暗自惊叹。

而现在我已有信心把它装进
口袋，像一盒火柴，可以照明，
可以取暖，可以做算命游戏。

but this is because I know

its strength. I've sensed it many times.

Similarly, I never worry about

questions of visibility and the like: I've noticed

a post office floating in its belly.

Just like that, three meals a day, take strolls at night,

read a few pages of Pascal before bed.

The window's open. I've felt the change.

Because of this, I was for a time most engrossed

with where its edges lay,

this always left me full of secret wonder.

But now I have the confidence to stuff it

in a pocket like a box of matches, good for a light,

good for warmth, or for a fortune-telling game.

并且我允许它变作一只蚂蚁

溜出来,看着它从我的手臂

钻进我的胸膛,我承认,痒——

你掀开我灵魂九曲连环的入口,

而这正像我始终好奇的那样:当我

看见你时,我已在你之中。

I also let it turn into an ant and

slip out, watch it cross my arm,

burrow into my chest where, I admit, it tickles –

You have opened the labyrinthine entrance to my soul

and, as curious as I've always been: when I see you

I am already within you.

(tr. by Heather Inwood)

小夜曲
——为 X·Y 而作

血在血管里流得多么慢
仿佛心脏已经是石头
露出水面的部分
长满了苔藓

停电了。一截短短的蜡烛
在纸面上放下一个桔子
颤抖的边缘
像黑暗的牙痛

此时,一扇失修的门
正在音乐厅里熟睡
并且,在人已走光的梦中
断断续续地,鼓着掌

Serenade
——for X.Y.

Blood flows so slowly in my veins
it seems my heart is a stone
and the part that sticks out of the water
is covered over with lichen.

Power outage. A candle stub
deposits a tangerine on the paper,
the edges shiver
like the twilight's toothache.

Right now, a rickety door
is fast asleep in the concert hall
and in the dreams of those who've left
is an intermittent clapping.

What my fingers touch

我的手指触到的

是夜的残缺的、温暖的驼背

是另一方消失后的通话中

仍然竖着的那副听筒

is the night's warm, damaged humpback,

it's the telephone still held

after the conversation has vanished.

(tr. by Eleanor Goodman)

黄茜 Huang Qian

黄茜，诗人，毕业于北京大学外国语学院世界文学所，现供职于南方都市报社。出版诗集《女巨人》等，曾获北京大学未名诗歌奖和刘丽安诗歌奖"。

Huang Qian, Chinese poet, graduated from the Institute of World Literature, College of Foreign Languages at the Beijing University, currently working at *Southern Metropolis Daily*. She published a poetry collection: *The Giantess* and won Weiming Poetry Prize from the Beijing University and Liu Lian Poetry Prize.

七年 / Seven Years

回忆细成腕间银链

诱捕悠游鱼群

他的脸还藏在深梦中

偶尔教她哀哭

偶尔夜空骤然反转

她承不住漫天倾倒的恶心

扑落于巉岩翅下

偶尔她醒来在明亮湖边

赤红与银白的花朵环绕小岛

Memories molt to a silver chain on the wrist

a netted shoal of leisurely fish

his face is still hidden in dreams

sometimes teaching her misery

sometimes suddenly reversing in the night

she can't bear the toppling nausea

that scatters down from the wings of crags

sometimes she wakes beside a shining lake

crimson and silvery flowers surround a small island

and her thoughts are utterly silent

思绪静不可测

有时她绝望地感到

他的力量

如同咒语，如同碾碎思想的

力，她愿变成风筝或者

阴影。有时她沉默注视

他与他的世俗心

在长夜小酒馆蓄着

浓香，在阴天与晴天

隐遁窗与水晶言辞之后

放牧厌世者的轻佻

她像个

追逐闪电的孩子

知道瞬息与永恒的悖论

流丽诗句是火的刻印

夜的沼泽中，拔起

细瘦脚踝，甜柔的歌者

her despair at times makes her feel

his power

like a curse, like the pulverized power

of thought, and she wants to become a kite

or a shadow. At times she silently watches

him and his ordinary heart

gathering its strong scent all night

in a bar, and between clouds and sun

after a reclusive window and crystalline words

there's the frivolity of a pessimist put out to pasture

she resembles

a child chasing lightning

knowing the paradox of ephemeral and eternal

beautiful poetry is an engraving of fire

pulling up a delicate ankle

from the bog of the night, a tender singer

used up by an admonition

the endless polishing and revising

消耗于对一句箴言

无尽润色与编撰

她偶尔在倾斜宇宙中疾飞，而

银链是她的牢狱

(2010)

she sometimes flies falteringly in the tilting cosmos, but
the silver chain is her prison.

(2010)

死亡路过二十六年

死亡路过二十六年
悲哀的湖，铅色的骨头
开出冶艳的花朵。幻觉在空气里
轻颤，我听见上帝的声音
围捕了上千只火鸟，
走投无路的少女在碎石峰顶
双臂在风中狂乱地书写：
爱——
苍白的水草自水面站起
它们缠住月色
和溺死者的脚踝，多么冰凉骷髅的
铃声，自深海渗入忍痛的
泪腺。最终，蔓延的伤口蚕食了身体，
她疯转的灵魂，在漩涡
和不育的矿石上跳舞——
亲爱者手擎反讽之镜，世人却在
另一端沉沦。

(2010)

The Dead Pass Through Twenty-Six Years

The dead pass through twenty six years

a grieving lake, leaden bones

flowers in smoldering colors. Delusions shiver

in the air, I hear the voice of God

netting thousands of phoenixes,

and a young girl at an impasse on a shattered-stone summit

writes madly in the air with her arms:

Love—

pale water reeds stand up from the water

they entangle the moonlight

and the ankles of the drowned, clinking of the frigid

skeletons, and oceanic tear glands seeping

into a dignified pain. At last, the spreading wound eats at the body,

and her crazily spinning soul, in a whirlpool

or on sterile ore, dances—

the beloved's hand props up a satirical mirror, and on the other side

the people descend into sin.

(2010) (tr. by Eleanor Goodman)

王璞　Wang Pu

王璞（1980—），诗人、译者，生于山西，长于北京，纽约大学文学博士，现执教于美国布兰德斯大学。曾获北京大学未名诗歌奖、刘丽安诗歌奖、诗东西诗歌奖。

Wang Pu, Chinese poet & translator, born in 1980 in Shanxi, raised in Beijing, currently teaches at Branders University, USA, with PhD in Literature at New York University. He is the winner of several poetry awards including Weiming Poetry Prize at the Beijing University, Liu Lian Poetry Prize and DJS-Poetry East West Prize.

宝塔
────给李春及一代人

宝塔亦是蜡烛。树边的湖

和湖畔的酒瓶，从中取暖。

宝塔为什么不是酒瓶呢？

你举起来，是要再饮一口？

是吹瓶哨？还是将它投入湖中，

扯开嗓子向夜生活一唱？

大我，小我风驰电掣。宝塔

The Reliquar
────For Li Chun and His Contemporaries

The reliquary is a candle; the lake by the trees

And the bottle on its shore, drawing on its warmth.

And why isn't it the bottle ?

You raise it, perhaps to take another drink ?

To whistle ? Or cast it into the lake,

Rending your lungs in song to the night life.

I, myself, gallop swift as storm winds, the reliquary

Rising abruptly from weekend shopping receipts to

忽然从周末的购物清单上立起来,说:爱!
仇恨!你的右手摸索的,不像是
鼠标或西文书,而是窗棂:推开吧,
让翻译的细雾进来。山形在多语中浮现,
犹如磨砂面的曙光——太伪劣!如此背景下

宝塔是险峰。你转而握住的黑暗,
总是它的倒影。宝塔于是向左看齐。
向你看齐。它可以是毛茸茸的,果味儿的,荧
　　光的。
但首先是红色的。

proclaim: Love!

Hate! That with which your right hand fumbles, resembles
Not a computer mouse or western book, but a window frame: Push it open,
Let in the fine vapours of translation. Mountain forms rising from the babble,
A sandpaper dawn —So false! Against this backdrop

The reliquary stands a pinnacle; the darkness you turn to grasp,
Forever its reflection. Eyes left in attention,
Its gaze follows you. Although it may be gossamer soft, fruit flavoured, fluorescent,
Above all else it's crimson.

有关声音

舞曲又重放了一次。一个塑料歌手
半裸在天花板中央。它的节奏
把上紧的发条挤进了温室之中,
而且,吻合了最新的宿命,训练者人们
喝咖啡,进食,交谈,各怀心思,
自信地行走——每个动作都合拍,
散发出规范的迷人芬芳。

服务员按动按钮时蹦出的提示音,
仿佛在呼唤我灵魂中的幽暗丝绒。
"您的冰激凌,您的汉堡,
您的结局。"——多熟练!
这时,不远处自编的手机铃声响起,
竟打破了那女子黑色上衣内
双乳间的大多数小秘密。

On Sound

The dance starts over, plastic singer
Half naked at the centre of the ceiling. The rhythm
Crams coiled springs in hothouses,
Chiming with the latest fate; instructing people
To drink their coffee, eat, converse, be pensive
And stride out – Each motion in step,
Exuding the heady scent of standards.

As the waiter pushes a button an announcement
   blares out,
Summoning the velvet darkness of my soul.
"Your ice-cream Sir, your hamburger,
Sir, your ending." – And all so polished!
Then, nearby, from under her black coat
A young woman's custom ring tone resounds,
Shattering for the greater part the small secrets of her
   cleavage.

Oh, only the vulgar would remark,

归巢与启程
中澳当代诗选（中国卷）
Homings and Departures—Selected Poems from Contemporary China and Australia

哦，唯有粗心者才会发现，

唱歌的天使正纷纷飞去，

长袍的簌簌声。

泪的雾，雾的韵。我试图挽留他们，但

一开口就是敲打键盘的低诉——

等等！这刺耳的是什么，突然涌入神经？

是某个点起的纠错声，还是我的心脏在疼痛地

　　报时？

Angels taking flight in flurried chorus,

Robes bristling.

Mists of tears, rhythms of mists, I urge them to
　　remain yet

Opening my mouth, all that comes out is the hushed
　　complaint of tapping keys—

But wait! That awful noise, so sudden an influx on
　　the nerves?

Is it the error message of some device? Or my heart,
　　painedly proclaiming the hour?

(tr. by Ali McInnes)

赵四 Zhao Si

赵四，70后诗人，现为《诗刊》编辑，《当代国际诗坛》副主编。出版诗集《白乌鸦》《消失，记忆：2009-2014新诗选》等。

Zhao Si, post-70 poet, editor of *Poetry Periodical* and the Executive Editor-in-Chief of the prestigious poetry translation series *Contemporary International Poetry*. She is the author of several poetry collections including *White Crow*, *Disappearing and Recalling: 2009 - 2014 New Selected Poems*.

孩子

他们消失了，转眼
无踪。海浪涌动，卷走的时间
一个个打着卷的涡旋，卷发柔软，
笑容明亮。

明亮的他们消失了，成片成片。此前
他们是星星，在地球上黯淡的反光
Cherubim，借用了灵魂最初的模样
反光双翼的量子波长

Children

They disappeared, swiftly

without a trace. Coiling waves, whirled-away time,

each and every spinning vortex, soft curling hair,

bright smiles.

Acres and acres vanished, they of brightness. Before

they were dim reflections of stars on the earth.

Cherubim, borrowed the initial appearance of the

    soul,

the quantum fluctuations of their light-reflecting

    wings;

但星星们离地球太远
反光震荡

打着卷的时间,柔软的天使
反光消失了,消失得太快。

stars, too far away from the earth,
reflection fluctuates.

Coils and coils whirled-away time, soft angels,
the reflections of stars disappeared, so swift.

叹息
——为大屠杀死难者

我听见，我听见掉进混乱与惊恐的人群
掠起群集的雨乌鸦，大笑，成群的大笑飞过
撞着哭墙。胜利的业火口含利刃
切割叹息，一片，两片，羽毛飞舞
你出现，出现在漫天大雪中
你们所无法想象的事物出现，时间到了
白色的血滴滴溅起，雪花中最亮的朵朵
我看见，我看见你的大苦之心鼓胀，鼓胀
轰然而出的天使，一边敛紧他尚不熟悉的
大翼翅的根部，顶住从你的内心吹出的风口
一边用尖嘴喙低头凿开偌大的石化世界
已经僵硬的你，如此巨大的叹息矗立内燃
一堵火墙，一堵火墙阴湿地燃烧，冒着
苦涩的白烟坍塌，埋下，埋下永恒叹息

Sighs
—For All the Slaughter Victims

I hear, I hear the flock of rain, crowing, rushing out of stirred
crowds of chaos and fright, sweeping past, laughing, roars of
laughter crashing into the Wailing Wall. Triumphant karma
holds a sharp blade in its mouth and slices the sigh into
pieces; one piece, two pieces feathers flutter, dancing.
You emerge, among the whirling sleet
The thing, the mortals can't imagine arises. It's time
drops of white blood splash, the brightest blossom of solid
    snowflakes.
I see, I see your heart of great suffering swells up, up
till an angel thunders out, and he flexes up the roots
of his not-yet-familiar large wings, pressing against the gust
blowing from the gap in the heart, then bows his head to
    peck
such an immense petrified world with his sharp beak.
An already rigid You giant sigh, stands upright, burning
inside.
A fire wall, a wall of fire burns darkly and damply, smoking
whitely and bitterly, collapses and buries, buries the eternal
    sighs.

(tr. by Xuan Yuan & Tim Lilburn)

戴潍娜　Dai Weina

戴潍娜，80后诗人，毕业于牛津大学，中国人民大学博士，现就职于中国社科院文学研究所。出版诗集《面盾》《灵魂体操》等。

Dai Weina is a post-80s poet, scholar, working for the Chinese Academy of Social Sciences in Beijing. She holds an MPhil from Oxford University and a PhD from the Renmin University of China. She has authored four poetry collections, notably *Face Shield* and *Spirit Gymnastics*.

塑料做的大海

最后一次呼吸闭眼停止换气。我练习消失
是蓝色，蓝得太假，像一圈浅蓝色的塑料板
塑料做的大海，塑料做的誓言
我终于赤足走在我意念构建的世界
这里天荒地老每日发生，相爱是生存法则

海豚是飞的，外面的人类还在爬行
椰子树撅起的肥臀露着妊娠纹
我一不小心爱上坠落沙地的
笨重的花，过马路发呆的小蜥蜴，天花板中央

Plastic Sea

For the last time, eyes closed, I breathe and stop breathing.
　I practice disappearing.
It's blue, too blue to be true, like a circle of light-blue
　plastic boards.
Plastic sea. Plastic vows.
I'm finally walking barefoot in the world constructed by
　my ideas,
where eternal love, a survival rule, happens every day.

Dolphins are flying. The humans outside still crawling
Coconut trees stick out their fat butts, revealing gravidity
　lines.

的壁虎探子
和露天马桶上的红蚂蚁
热带总是这样感情凶猛,天公打雷如打嗝儿
我意识到需要创造一个爱我的男人,在盛满海水的浴缸旁
怯生生递上白毛巾,证明我的此刻
又是一个不小心,我把他造得太老了,风都刮不动
会落泪的,温柔的老年斑
我说扮上吧,海水中央有一座大戏台——你过去
换上沙丁鱼的皮肤和关公蟹的凶器
这样你就能刺破我制造的幻象,回到真实
我会收回这一切,把日夜折叠,把大海灌进高脚杯
杯子里全是蓝色。一世界的蓝色。真得太假
塑料做的大海,塑料做的誓言
蓝色,蓝色

(2013)

I accidentally fall in love with the unwieldy flowers dropping on the sands, the dazed little lizards crossing the road, the geckos spying at the center of the ceiling, the red ants on the open-air toilet.
In the tropics filled with wild emotions, thunder sounds like a belch.
I realize I have to create a man who loves me, who timidly hands over a white towel beside a bathtub of seawater, to prove my presence.
Accidentally again, I make him too old, even the wind can't move those tender, tear-shedding age spots.
I say, Dress up, there's a grand stage in the sea – go there
And put on the sardine's skin and the musk-crab's pincers
in so doing you can pierce the illusion I created and return to reality.
I will take back all this, folding up days and nights, and pour the sea into a goblet.
All blue in the glass. A world of blue. Too real to be true.
Plastic sea. Plastic vows.
Blue. Blue.

(2013) (published in The Lifted Brow, Australia)

仰光情人

你的头脑负责体验一切噩梦
你的身体负责美梦

打开你的冰柜,打开你白色胸衣
打开两片干净的肺页
如推开一扇百叶窗
把鼓点敲进你腔肠
把信冻进冰箱

我只有十一个情人
我只有诗一个情人

软甜奶酪中泡澡的 Darling
为了你,我什么都可以

当我们相爱的时候

Rangoon Lover

Your mind is to taste all nightmares.
Your body in charge of fond dreams.

Open your icebox, your white bra.
Open the two clean lungs
like you push open the shutters.
Knock the drumbeats into your guts.
Freeze the letters in a fridge.

I only have eleven lovers.
I only have poetry, this one lover.

My darling bathing in soft cheese:
for you, I can even join the Party.

When we are in love,
we don't do anything legal.

As you breathe out *chit pa de*,

违法的事儿我们不干

当你要吐出 chit pa de

小鸟啄走了字母

你写我，我写你

(2014)

a bird pecks them away.

You write about me, I about you.

(2014) (tr. by Liang Yujing, published in The Poetry Review, UK)

康苏埃拉 Consuela

康苏埃拉,诗人,现居旧金山,从事艺文类翻译出版与写作。曾获未名诗歌奖、重唱诗歌奖和樱花诗歌奖。
Sufei "Consuela" Yang is a poet and translator based in San Francisco. She has won a series of poetry awards in Mainland China, including Weiming Poetry Prize, Chongchang Poetry Prize and Yinghua Poetry Prize.

尽管火种并不忠诚
——致一位诗人

海滨的守火人食字,也偶尔饮海
尽管火种并不忠诚
但你熟识热带,这么多
不可逾越的纬度,这么多通红的眼睛
你站在里面捕捞辞藻,
用直觉的斧子砍柴。
而那片被划分出内外的水域仿佛某种决定:
一旦搭建,就意味着劈开。

Though the Fire's Faith Is Yet Wavering
—To a Poet

The fire-keeper by the shore eats words, and occasionally sips
    from the sea.
Although the fire's faith is yet wavering,
Long enough have you known for this tropical scene. All these
Latitudes beyond your reach. All these eyes winkling crimson
In the midst of which you spread net wide for some rhetoric,
chopping wood by an axe by an institutional edge.
And ever the body of water split apart, eventually converge
    into a decision:

现在，守火的人请告诉我

如果今天还不是时候，

那么是不是就在明晚？

在鲸歌响起的海上

你将拾回第一粒盐——

总有一捧焦土还留有远祖的姓氏

写下它，使我的燃烧像海一样开始。

Once built, the world is meant to be cleaved up again .

Now please inform me, the keeper of fire:

If today is not our time,

Will it be tomorrow night ?

Through the mountain waves aroused by a whale song-

Will salt's birh poace you retrace in remote antiquity.

Of all scorched earth still there is one last land dusted with our
 primary name.

Write it down and let the burning of me startup, violently with
 the wild sea.

缺席即永在

你不在这个黄昏，不在
与鸽群有关的颤音之间，替我熄灭
雪，熄灭一场死雪纷飞的叫喊。

你也不在宇宙心里，紧握这束渐红的时辰
敲着同样渐红的我，因赤裸
而未能敲响的大门。

你不在那扇门外，不在它已到达的
一切暗穴，也不在我的半空
那些比意义更野蛮的焰火之中。

你不在这簇词语，迸裂
闪着光亮的末节，也不在它们体内
黑与黑的间隙。

The Absent and the Everlasting

You do not show yourself in this sunset. Nor among
The fluttering of doves, to extinguish an upcoming
Snow, or to quench dead snowflakes' scream for me.

Nor do you dwell in heart of our universe, grip to a
    burst of rosy hours
Or knock at the door that has refused to open for
The reddening me, way too naked for my presence.

Clearly, you do not linger around to that entrance,
    or even to the lair
Hidden by its other end. Nor rise up to my midair,
converging your life into brutal flames among the
    meanings of it all.

You do not dive in this whole cluster of words, not
    in my

你不在此时，此刻，只在你——
因被我称之为罂粟而灼伤的唇上
在唇的创痛所能触及，一整片
对其他事物广阔的摧毁里。

Torn-up yet vaguely glimmering syllables. Nor deep
 enough
To reach the cracks between the darkness within.

You never submit yourself to this moment, this
 instant, but only cast a shadow
On your deep burnt lips which I would call a pair of
 poppies
And on the pain they would ever reach— the
 boundless ruin
Upon existence's traces of all other things.

      (tr. by the auther & Ametia Date)

张定浩 Zhang Dinghao

张定浩（1976–），诗人，出版诗集《我喜爱一切不彻底的事物》等，现为《上海文化》杂志副主编。
Zhang Dinghao, Chinese poet, born in 1976, is the author of poetry collection: *I Love All Incomplete Things*, currently working as the Deputy Chief Editor of *Shanghai Culture*.

1825 年 12 月 14 日   December 14, 1825

我看见他们站成一个个方阵，
在枢密院广场，
严肃、庄重、如此年轻，
相信沉默的力量。

连卢克莱修都可以解释，
他们在寒冷的十二月，
聚集于此的原因，
不过是起始于

I see them stand in those even phalanxes
on Senate Square,
committed, un-amused – too young
to be pushing this silent engine.

Even Lucretius could explain why,
here in bitter December,
they have collected here,
is it merely because of

the random shifting of some atoms,

一些原子的自由偏移，

一个简单的物理现象，

不必紧张，不必紧张，

即使他们冲进枢密院，

即使沙皇被撕成风中的碎片。

然而，什么都没有发生，

唯有沉默的方阵以及

大片飘落的雪花以及

额头缓缓凝固的汗水。

可是喧嚣声已临近，

炮兵正点燃引信，

酒馆里的人群也纷纷走上大街，

好像要提前迎接

圣子的降临。

我看见大雪中均匀呼吸的他们

正如春天里轻轻振翅的蝴蝶，

a mundane physical phenomenon,

don't be afraid don't be afraid,

even should they charge the Senate building,

even should they tear the tsar into quilt scraps.

And yet – nothing, beyond

the wordless phalanx, and

the fat snowflakes drifting, and

beads of sweat congealing on their foreheads.

But the voice of chaos is already near,

the grenadiers have lit their fuses,

The crowd at taverns have filtered into the street

as if prematurely preparing

to receive God's son.

I see them, their chests rise and fall regularly in the blizzard

like a butterfly moves its wings in spring,

how utterly unaware,

that they're the cause of a tropical tornado .

它们茫然不知，
自己会是一场热带风暴的源头。

天色开始发暗，
在遮羞布徐徐拉合之前，
黑色旋涡的中央，
有一只蝴蝶嘶哑着歌喉，
他们静静地听。

(2002)

The sky begins to glower
as the loincloth calmly comes together
at the center of the black whirlpool,
a butterfly shouts a hoarse melody
to which they quietly listen.

(2002)

纸箱子

你一定还记得那些捆扎结实的纸箱子。
汛期来临的时候,它们漂浮于每一条楼道,
像男孩子们手里的船模,轻盈而坚固。
这曾让人觉得安心,
因为我只有两只手,你也一样,
不能带走一切。

可我能不能告诉你,我正听见
它们不断下沉的声音?
而原以为它们会顺流直下的,
以为它们会先我们一步,
抵达桃源的深处,早早准备好无数
令人唏嘘的礼物。

我能不能告诉你它们正在沉没,
正穿过幽暗的水藻,

Cardboard Boxes

I know you remember those bound-up cardboard
   boxes.
When the spring tide came, they floated in every
   hallway,
light and rigid, like the model ships boys carry.
This once brought me peace,
as I have only two hands, as do you,
we can't take it all.

But may I tell you, how I can hear
the sound of them sinking ?
though we had thought they would ride the current,
go before us, all the way to the deep eddies,
of paradise, and prepare for us
countless tearful gifts.

May I tell you they are disappearing,
dropping through purple kelp
and schools of migratory fish, through whirlpools

穿过迁徙的鱼群和漩涡，

以及一层层绵软如糖的流沙？

我能不能告诉你，

它们正静静地躺在我身边，

而一切都不曾被毁灭，

它们只是从水面消失？

(2004)

and layer on layer of candy-delicate sand ?

May I tell you

they now lie wordlessly beside me; and that

nothing ever was destroyed,

but simply gone from the water's surface ?

(2004) (tr. by Canaan Morse)

肖水　Xiao Shui

肖水（1980–），诗人，生于湖南郴州，曾就读于复旦大学法学院、中文系。出版诗集《失物认领》《中文课》《艾草》《渤海故事集》，曾获北京大学未名诗歌奖、《上海文学》诗歌新人奖等。

Xiao Shui, Chinese poet, born in Chenzhou, Hunan Province in 1980, currently studies at the Faculty *of law* and the Department of Chinese at the Fudan University. He is the author of several poetry collections including *Lost Property Office*, *Chinese Lesson*, *Wormwood* and *Gulf of Bohai*. He is the winner of several poetry awards including Beijing University Weiming Poetry Award and New Poet Award of *Shanghai Literature*.

我们的粮食不多了

我们的粮食不多了

我不得不

向你陈述时代的遭遇

玉米，麦子，马铃薯

稻谷，我们赖以生存

但从不去生产的东西

饥饿像你未曾见过的烟花

饥饿是明天赐予今天的粮食

但乘天还没有全黑

Our Grain Is Running Out

Our grain is running out

We have to

pour out, for you, our encounters of the times.

corn, wheat, potatoes and

grains are the things we live on

but don't produce ourselves.

Hunger is like the fireworks you've not seen;

hunger is the food bestowed upon today by tomorrow.

Yet while night is yet to fall fully

sinking sun not sunk and mountains black,

say not that this is the last banquet

归巢与启程

中澳当代诗选（中国卷）
Homings and Departures—Selected Poems from Contemporary China and Australia

夕阳没落，群山黝黑一片

不要说这是最后的宴会

需要盛装和旗袍

不要说刀叉和餐盘

还在工匠的炉火中打造

乘月光还没有到来，我们

还可以做一次机会主义者

我们还可以将双脚踏入

南方秋天的稻田，和

稻田上空突然来袭的暴风雨

总会有路途通向遥远的粮仓

总会有抢劫者和暴怒的法官

总会有棺木和赞美的诗行

总会有从睡眠中惊醒的稻穗

它从老鼠偷取的家当里

它从农民不再吟唱的歌谣里

它从乞丐稀疏的手缝里

它与祖先的魂灵一起飞升，然后

降落在一块湿润的文字里

requiring evening dress and cheongsam;

say not that knife, fork and plate

are still being fired in the kiln.

While moonlight is not coming, we,

again, may play the Opportunist

might plant our feet into

southern grain fields in autumn,

tempest suddenly beating down on the fields.

There will be a road leading always to the remote barn;

there will be always a robber and a furious judge
   always;

there will always be a coffin and always praising poems;

there will always be eared grains awakened from sleep.

From stolen belongings of the mice,

from folk songs never sung by farmers,

from gaps between the fingers of beggars,

it soars with the souls of ancestors, and, just then,

lands on a field of humid words.

All along night, including darkness,

it bestows sleepiness and ennui, and we are waiting for.

the germination of a Chinese character and word.

一整个晚上,包括黑暗

赋予困倦,我都在等待

一个汉字和一个词的发芽

不待它开花,长成

杜甫胡须上的伟大诗句

李白酒杯里的澄清月光

我就拾起,并且迅速塞进嘴里

我们的粮食不多了

我向时间伸出双手

我知道,我比粮仓更加饥饿

更加困倦,使你要为我而哭

(2003)

Before it blossoms and grows up to

be the poems on Du Fu's beard, or.

be the bright moonlight in Li Bai's cup,

I pick it up and quickly tuck it into my mouth.

Our grain is running out.

I reach my hands out to time,

and I know I'm more hungry and exhausted

than that barn, which makes you cry for me.

(2003)　(tr. by Philip Fang & a.j carruthers)

渤海故事集（选二）

末日物候

那时候我们一家住在库区，父亲是附近林场的伐木工，
母亲经营着小杂货店，她经常要去县城进货，有时候回来晚了，
渡船开到湖心，会停掉马达，静静飘着。岸边漫山遍野都是白鹭，
被淹没的民居偶尔从水底露出来，上面挂满了湿滑的水草。

在冬天

他在大街上，掏出打火机，犹豫了一会儿，
终于把它点燃。接着，他拿出手机，对准火焰

Gulf of Bohai (excepts)

Apocalyptic Phenology

When our family lived near the reservoir, my father was a lumberjack in a nearby forest,
my mother ran a small grocery store, often going to the country to replenish stock, sometimes returning late,
when the ferry sailed to the center of the lake, the motor would stop, and it drifted quietly. The surrounding banks and plains,
were covered with white egrets, submerged houses, covered with slippery waterweeds, sometimes appeared on the bottom.

In Winter

On the street, he took out his lighter, slightly

的中心。

被放大的光,晃荡一下,几乎舔着了他的左手。

他想了想自己是怎么走到武东路的,车流里似乎真的有水声。

(2015)

hesitated,and finally lit it. Then, he took out his cell phone,and aimed at the flame's center.

The magnified light, sloshing, almost licked his left hand.

He contemplated how he got to Wudong Road, the traffic sounded like flowing water.

(2015) (tr. by Noelle Noéll)

胡桑　Hu Sang

胡桑（1981-），诗人，兼事文学批评，生于浙江新市，现任教于同济大学中文系。著有诗集《赋形者》，诗学论文集《隔渊望着人们》，译有《我曾这样寂寞生活：辛波斯卡诗选》。

Hu Sang, Chinese poet and critic, born in 1981, at Xinshi in Zhejiang Province, currently teaches at Tongji University in Shanghai. He is the author of several books including *The Former* (poetry collection), *Looking at People Across the Abyss* (poetic criticism), *I have such a lonely life: Poems of Wislawa Szymborska* (translation).

赋形者
——致小跳跳

尝试过各种可能性之后，

你退入一个小镇。雨下得正是时候，

把事物收拢进轻盈的水雾。

度日是一门透明的艺术。你变得

如此谦逊，犹如戚浦塘，在光阴中

凝聚，学习如何检测黄昏的深度。

The Shaper
—for Xiaotiaotiao

Having tried a number of possibilities,

You withdraw into a small town. It's raining at the right time;

The rain gathers everything into light fog.

Living your life is a transparent art. You become as humble

As the Qipu River you live beside. You hold yourself back

In time, and learn to measure the depth of dusk.

你出入生活，一切不可解释，从果园，
散步到牙医诊所，再驱车，停在小学门口，
几何学无法解析这条路线，它随时溢出。

鞋跟上不规则的梦境，也许有毒，
那些忧伤比泥土还要密集，但是你醒在
一个清晨，专心穿一只鞋子，

生活，犹如麦穗鱼，被你收服在
漆黑的内部。日复一日，你制造轻易地形式，
抵抗混乱，使生活有了寂静的形状。

我送来的秋天，被你种植在卧室里，
"返回内部才是救赎。"犹如柿子，
体内的变形使它走向另一种成熟。

You enter and exit life; most things cannot be
  explained
You wander from orchard to dentist, then drive,
To the gate of the schoolyard, a route
Unknown through geometry; it can overflow at any
  moment.

Irregular dreams on the heel might be toxic;
Sorrow is denser than clay, but you wake
In the morning, focused on wearing a shoe.

Like a flower-horn fish, your life is tamed
For a dark interior. Day by day, to counteract
  disorder,
And shape life into silence, you make an easy form.

Autumn has been planted in the bedroom.
  "Returning inward is redemption". Your body is
  transformed
Like a persimmon, and autumn has another kind of
  ripeness.

(tr. by the author & Brenda Hillman)

任性的人

窗外是城市，释放着争执的夜。初夏的薄雾
被吸入每一个人的肺部，它不懂得什么差别。
有时候我们只是忘记了：我们，来自不同的省份，
微凉的风，到底是无法修复身体与身体之间的
　　裂缝。

口音中的方言醒着，未闭合的铝合金窗醒着，
镜子在诉说着容忍，试图翻译人们的无知与傲慢，
桃浦西路已经认识了我，静默的大门却上着锁。
近处的桃浦河并不渴望什么，然而它醒着，醒着。

楼上，两个从不失眠的人促膝长谈，彻夜。
不为什么。大多数人活着，有时相互取悦，
有时相互伤害，于是，肉体醒来又睡去。
只有一封未拆的信，才能够守护那一团晦暗。

The Capricious

Beyond the window, the city sets loose contentious night,
late spring's mists inhaled by every lung, no exceptions.
Sometimes we forget we're from different regions,
yet this cool wind can't fill the gulf between our bodies.

Our accents rouse our dialects; windows wake in alloy frames.
Mirrors are at pains to translate ignorance, human arrogance.
Taopu West Road knows me well, though its silent gate stays shut.
The Taopu River, wanting nothing, never sleeps.

That couple upstairs, free of insomnia, talk heart-to-heart all night,
no reason. Most people sometimes please each other,
sometimes hurt. Bodies wake and sink asleep.
Only this letter, unopened, guards its dark packet.

(tr. Diana Shi & George O'Connell)

了小朱　Le Xiaozhu

了小朱（1986-），诗人，东方航空飞行员。
Le Xiaozhu, Chinese poet, born in 1986, currently serves as a pilot for China Eastern Airlines.

小淹留   Stranded a Little Longer

我在自己名下

建筑观念，如窗外鹅卵石

松松地闷死新夏的热门词

我去寻找现象

凭着一颗甜橙里的化学味

没想到人河已经流为运动

我白挤一身汗，抬手推开光

Concepts I build

under my name, like pebbles out of the window

smothering softly hot words of early summer

Phenomena I seek

by the taste of chemicals inside a sweet orange

heedless of the river of humans reduced to movement

In vain I sweat, pushing away the light

hiding in my sunglasses, humming under mucilage

at hotel's shop, a long nose bulges out of my throat

在墨镜中猫着，披着黏液哼

喉咙鼓出个长鼻子，酒店小卖店

木偶提线变作被测谎的丝丝沉思

我遇圆木，年轮藏着太平

孤独是千姿百态的支点

我不说话想去哪就去哪跌入伤疤里

在干冰天让语言知觉上冻

我最终是瘾者

露出夜班工人的机锋与古怪，还有已过春愁

双眼发病看到上个秋天的云覆有疾病的薄膜

我说预言不可能

计划在这个渐衰季，疯剪一批木本植物赏清秋

这些务虚的命令仿佛惹眼的神明

这个地区，不中用的象征要开练我的轻松人生

puppet strings become polygraphed thoughts

A log I encounter, its growth rings harbouring the peace
 solitude a fulcrum of various shapes
without a word, going wherever I wish until falling into
 the scar
letting feeling for language freeze in a day of dry ice

After all I'm an addict, like a night-shift-worker
awkward, trénchant, dismayed by the spring past
my ailing eyes glimpse a film of disease over last autumn's
 clouds

Impossible to predict, I say, so in the waning season
I'm planning to trim a batch of woody plants to enjoy the
 autumn
these empty orders are like conspicuous gods
in this area, all the futile symbols will usher in my easy life

(tr. by Sun Jie & & a.j carruthers)

经验之谈

诗歌是种特殊的耳疾
———奥登

雨忽然参与了打击

忘带晴雨计的人被问道

"你算什么关心政治的人"

他没料到潮气能如此绝对

就骗腿跳入地下通道

渴望抖落一身的过错

昏黄的吊灯下孤墙和他一起流汗

回应他的喃喃自语

"充其量是次貌似无边的轻侮"

路人暂时收起花伞

一瞥擦伤他护树人的胳膊

他侍弄森林多年

将陆续的信号传递给妻子

Voice of Experience

Verse was a special illness of the ear
———Auden

The rain suddenly joined the battle

He who forgot the barometer was asked

"How dare you call yourself a man on politics"

He never expected the moisture to be so absolute

So he jumped into the underpass

Yearning to shake off all mistakes

Under the pendant lamp's dim light, a lonely wall
    sweat with him

In response to his murmur

"It's at most, an insult seemingly immense"

A passer-by closed the umbrella for the moment

Glancing at the abraded arms of the park ranger

He has tended to the forest for many years

And sent intermittent signals to his wife

"Do not let the wind and rain in"

"别放那风雨进屋"

并没有提起折叠过的爱意

忧愁包裹住要狂舞的韵脚

只能跺着干巴巴地说

"他们的制度是奉献不讲条件"

但裸露伤痕又有何用

这老练的时间贼多亏了科技

才偷出那么多的新杂碎

快速消磨我们的日月

未来对我已然紧促

可对奇迹的出现仍不敏感

只能绕着暗泣的边缘

驱蝎一瞬走神就饮尽了光

"这是多么生动的论据"

为此曾尝试要割舍心灵

将伶仃之海凝于笔尖之上

薄水映照出桥顶的肋骨

由它的背全权把雷电滚过

Yet without a word on his folded love

The dancing rhyme was wrapped by melancholy

In the end it stamped, and said dryly

"Their regime favours devotion, not compensation"

Of what avail is displaying our wounds

This adroit thief of time used technology

To steal so many new scraps

That rapidly frittered away our days

The future was impelling

But I was not sensitive for its miracle

By the fringe, I sobbed in silence

Chased away the scorpions and drained the light
  instantly

"It is such a vivid argument"

For this, once I tried to give up my heart

The lonely sea coagulated on pen's tip

The thin water mirrored ribs of the bridge

Thunder and lightning rolled on its back

The summer heat made the entire city vomit

暑热使整个城市呕吐

却把飞行员拱上天

脚步让雨声更激动

只剩下最小可能的停顿

麻烦已经成形

如此震耳的声音是什么

如此清晰的闪光是什么

冲歪的石板颠荡我的细胞

"去，去发现灰烬的用途"

从雨帘中挤出身子

透气的时候浑身湿透

倒出悬壶里的水洗是非

"菌也要活得自由自在"

我的心蜷成一个铁球

对流行活生生的畏缩

说起这个是想告诉催眠人

"给生命作伪证的是你们"

Yet vaulted the pilot into the sky

Footsteps have stirred the rain even more

What remained was the shortest possible pause

Trouble was now formed to shape

What was that astounding voice

What was that distinct flash

The slabs were flushed askew, jolting my cells

"Go there, go find the use of ashes"

Drenched in the rain, the body

Cleaved out to breathe

I poured the water from the pot to clean disputes

"Even the fungus would like a free life"

My heart swirled like an iron ball

Fearful of what became popular

I mentioned this to inform the hypnotiser

"It is you who committed perjury for life"

The wind was chasing the weeping clouds

"Sky was not a strolling ground"

风还在赶含泪的云

"天空不是什么溜达中心"

它也吹过尘世里的女人

她们有的是松形的身体

逐渐不规范的内分泌

我听不懂有人在说什么

我有种病会耗尽年华

In this world, it has also blown through the women

Whose figures were flabby

With emerging endocrine disorders

I could not make sense of people's words

I had an illness that could wear out my years

(tr. by Sun Jie)

丝绒陨　Si Rongyun

丝绒陨（1985–），诗人，摄影师，现居上海。著有诗集《梦地察看》《八月的鲸鱼转让大海》《谁与我跳舞，谁就迷途》等。

Si Rongyun, Chinese poet and photographer, born in 1985, currently lives in Shanghai. He is the author of three poetry collections: *Dream Inspection, Whale in August Attorns the Sea,* and *Whoever Dances with Me Gets Lost.*

灰尘

满地跌落的橘子哭了，可是那年幼的
星星？点燃群梦里绵延的膏灯
但扑灯的蛾不吻便死去

傍晚携带顽童去河湾里游玩，要询问
在那心碎和潦倒的日子里，你
为什么一直谈论着灰尘

"我只知道人是人，灰尘是灰尘"

Dust

The tangerines cry as they fall on the ground, but
   what aboat those young
Stars ? the sprawling lamps in dreams ignite ,
yet the phototactic moths die without kissing .

In the evening I carry urchins to the rive and ask:
in those heart-breaking and frustrating days, why
did you keep talking about dust ?

' I only know that humans are humans, and dust is
   dust.'

"不，灰尘活着时是你

你死后是灰尘"

(2012)

'No, dust is you when you are alive

You are dust after death'

(2012)

童年玩伴 / Childhood Playmate

死，是另外一个孩子，瘦脸
有时会来找我玩，敲门，每次都是
三下，节制而规律，形成一种习惯
像他摘下帽子露出额头的痂——
一个被火星烫伤的奇怪标记，他说
他不怪罪每日在云里抽烟和在酒潭里
潜泳的爸爸，他老了，拴在柱子上
也不能归咎于久坐在梳妆台前叹息的
妈妈。他的家在湖对面的亚麻地深处
我竟然从没有真正到那里看过
（我往那个方向去过几次，没到达就
折返回来）也不能亲眼见到他所描述的
古旧摆设，保持在各自的恰当位置
有时我还没起床，他趴在睡袋口
看着我；有时我碰巧在厨房喝牛奶
会有羽毛从窗口飘入，说起来

Death, is another child, with a thin face
Occasionally he comes to play with me, knocks three times,
moderate and regular, forming a habit
Like the scar on his forehead that is uncovered when he takes off his hat –
It's a strange mark burnt by Mars, he says
He doesn't blame his father who smoked every day in clouds
and swam in alcohol, who was old, tied to the post
nor his mother who sat and sighed
at her dresser. His home was in the depths of the flax field across the lake
Unexpectedly, I have never really been there to have a look
(I have headed towards there several times, but returned
Before arriving) or to see the antique furnishings
he described, kept in their proper positions
Sometimes when I am not yet up, he lays prone in the sleeping bag
looking at me; sometimes when I happen to be drinking milk in the kitchen
there are feathers floating in from the window,

他总是收集些类似这样古怪的小物件

寡言的鸟，不能骑的衰老马匹

不再保鲜的鱼罐头，他大概爱这些

苔藓覆盖的事物，不喜光，背阴

不再期待生长成凶猛的形状

"太阳落山前必须回家"出门前，妈妈

总这样叮嘱。于是我们快跑着穿过前厅

穿过一些间断的小水洼，来到

停着废弃驳船的芦苇地，原来

水洼与水洼之间是这样连接的

你取下帽子给我看你的痂

你甚至从怀中抱出猫来，说这是魔术

出于敬佩，也出于自尊，我说

这没什么好奇怪的，我还曾经把一只

斑斓的老虎抱在怀里呢，又亲手把他

放生。这时一只野鹧鸪飞过头顶

沿着发光的曲线你去追逐

仿佛热爱一种坠落，你跑起来像是

海水涨潮，水洼渐吞没芦苇地

something to speak of
He always collects quaint baubles such as
a silent bird, a doddery horse which cannot be ridden,
Some canned fish that aren't fresh, he probably loved these things
covered in moss in the shade, not heliophilous,
he did not expect them to grow into feral shapes
Before leaving, mum always warned, 'You have to be home before the sun sets.'
Then we rushed across the front hall
Across some sporadic puddles, and arrived at
The reeds where discarded barges were moored, so that was how one puddle joined another
You took off your hat to show me your scar
You even took a cat out of your arms, saying it was magic
Out of admiration, and of self-esteem, I said
This is nothing surprising, once I even held a
Colourful tiger in my arms, and let it go
with my hands. Just now a wild francolin flies over head
and you go chasing the luminous curve
As if you love falling, you run like
the rising tide, puddles gradually swallowing up the reed field

它消失，像一片无辜的海滩被浪吃掉
空手而归，你摊开双手，一脸悲伤
"人们总说要去远方跳一支舞，但也
总是不知要去哪里，有时又去得太远
忘记回家。"每当这时就意味着告别了
我抬头看看水洼，水洼发育而成的湖
湖那边烈火烧过的云髻，他的家
他说那不过是另一个标记，和额头上的
一样。我于是踏着并不连贯的水花
独自走回来，而我年少孤独的玩伴
总是背道而驰

(2012)

It disappears, like an innocent beach gobbled up
   by the waves
Coming back empty-handed, you spread out your
   hands, shadowed with sorrow,
'People always talk about going somewhere far
   away to dance, but they
Never know where to go, or sometimes go too far,
Forgetting to come back home.' At times like this,
   it means goodbye
I look at the puddles, the lake that has formed
The flaming clouds over it, and his home
He said it was only another mark, the same as the
   one
On his forehead. Then I stepped and splashed about
   here and there
Strolled back home alone, while my young solitary
   playmate
Always ran into the opposite direction.

(2012) (tr. by Gu Yiwei & Cassandra Atherton)

包慧怡　Bao Huiyi

包慧怡（1985–），生于上海，爱尔兰都柏林大学中世纪文学博士，复旦大学中澳创意写作中心副主任。出版诗集《我坐在火山的最边缘》《异教时辰书》，专著 The Pearl-Poet and the Sensorium in Medieval England，《中古英语抒情诗的艺术》等。

Bao Huiyi, born in Shanghai in 1985, PhD in Old and Middle English Literature at University College Dublin, is currently vice director of the China–Australia Creative Writing Centre, the Fudan University. She has published two books of poetry, *A Pagan Book of Hours* and *I Sit on the Edge of the Volcano*; two monographs, *The Pearl-Poet and the Sensorium in Medieval England* and *The Art of Middle English Lyrics*.

岛屿生活

这是冰川时代遗留的
巨型圆丘，这是淡金色山谷拥戴的
灰蓝峡湾，这是圣灰树
正顶风炫耀逝者缤纷的许愿结
这是一场久远饥荒后废弃的牧场。

从一座岛到另一座，选择永远是假象
从一片海到另一片，维京人心知肚明
所以蓄长须，削龙骨，从容劈开雪鬃怒浪

The Archipelago

Here are mossy mounds left over
from the glacial epochs, here are dusty blue fjords
in pale gold valleys. Here is an ash tree
showing off the gaily colored wish knots of the departed
and here is a pasture abandoned in a famine long ago.

From one island to another, choice is an illusion.
From ocean to ocean, the Vikings knew it well.
Braid your beards, fix your keels, split the snow-white surf:
You'd have to be as barren and warlike as these retreating
　waves
to call it conquest—the islanders never think of it that way.

你得好斗又贫瘠，像节节败退的泡沫高墙
才会管那叫征服——岛民们从不这么想。

他们熟知那白云，日日出没于西山
踯躅于崖畔：它不会改变形态，投身湖海；
他们眼中长草，细看焦石坡绵延，暗忖先祖们
也许来自蛾摩拉；死去国王的宝座列队
隐入浓雾与骤雨，那峭壁上独坐的老人

还吹响永不变奏的风笛。从一座岛到另一座
从无沾受孕的番石榴到化身绵羊的山蔷薇
奇迹是众岛的特产；从观看一幅画到成为画
成为颜料、天青石、山脉，成为布纤维和透视法
你愿知道的一切，岛屿都乐意吐露

但别指望真相。

They know these clouds well, climbing the same western
  hills,
lingering on that cliff: never changing, never diving into
  the waters.
Grass grows in their eyes as they gaze at the Burren,
  wondering
whether their ancestors came from Gomorrah. Thrones
  of dead kings
march off into the fog, an old man on the bluff

plays a changeless tune on the bagpipes. From one islet to
another,
from the immaculate guava to the sheep-impersonating
  gorse,
miracles are every island's specialty. From looking at a
  painting
to becoming one, becoming pigments, lapis, a mountain
  range, fabric and perspective
anything you want to know, the islands are willing to tell

except the truth.

关于抑郁症的治疗

现在,我只需把胸中的钝痛精细分辨
命名、加注、锁入正确的屉格:哪些眼泪是为
受苦的父亲而流,哪些为了染霜的爱,又有哪些
仅仅出于颤栗,为这永恒广漠、无动于衷的星
　　星监狱里
我们所有人的处境。假如每种精微的裂痛
都能像烦恼于唯识宗,找到自己不偏不倚的位置
像罪业于但丁的漏斗,它们将变得可以承受。

每种我不屑、不愿、不能倾诉的苦痛
都将郁结成棕色、橄榄色、水银色的香料
在时光的圣水瓶里酝酿一种奇迹。修辞术在受
　　难的心前
隐遁无踪,言语尽是轻浮,假如不是为了自救
铺陈不可饶恕。假如可以带粉笔进入迷宫,以
　　纯蓝

On Curing Depression

Now all I need to do is carefully differentiate
between each dull ache, name it, add a footnote,
　　lock it up
in the correct drawer: which tears I shed
for my suffering father, which for frostbitten love,
which came just from shivering in this vast,
　　indifferent
prison of stars in which we all live. If each small pain
could be precisely located, like troubles in Yogacara
　　buddhism,
they would, like sins in Dante's funnel, become
　　bearable.

Every pain I refuse to, won't stoop to, or simply
　　cannot pour out
will congeal into brown, olive, and silver spices
brewing miracles in the holy-water bottle of time.
Rhetoric evaporates before a suffering heart, speech
　　becomes frivolous ,

标记每一处通往灾祸的岔口:"我到过这儿
必将永不再受诱",它们将变得可以承受。

假如我尝过的每种汞与砷
能使你免于读懂这首诗
——它们将变得可以承受,
小病号。

and if not done in order to save oneself

narration is unforgivable. If I could take a piece of
   sky-blue chalk

into this maze, and mark every forking

that leads to disasters: "I have been here, I will not

be tempted again" then they would become
   bearable.

If all my tastes of mercury and arsenic

could exempt you from understanding this poem

—they would become bearable,

little patient.

(tr. by Austin Woerner & Bao Huiyi)

秦三澍 Qin Sanshu

秦三澍（1991– ），诗人，生于江苏徐州，现在巴黎高等师范学院攻读文学博士学位。著有诗集《比地图更远》，曾获柔刚诗歌奖、DJS– 诗东西诗歌奖、《人民文学》紫金之星奖等。

Qin Sanshu, Chinese poet, born in 1991 in Xuzhou, Jiangsu Province, currently is the PhD candidate at French literature the Ecole Normale Supérieure. He is the author of the poetry collection, *Farther than the Map*. He is the winner of the Rou-Gang Poetry Prize, the Young Poets' Prize, DJS–Poetry East West Prize and the Zi–Jin Prize of *People's Literature*.

低空

不会更高，是失去海拔的夜空，
是距离，从按门铃的指尖
压住深陷于食物的发烫的勺。

是让人担忧的餐具散出冷光，
把双份的病症，搅拌进数月后
咳喘着向我们举步的雪地里。

是勺子用金属的舌头卷起

Low Altitude

It won't get any higher. It is night-sky approaching
    sea-level
it is distance, from the finger pushing the doorbell
to the hot spoon pressing its divot in the food.

It is cold light scattered from unsettling cutlery,
a double portion of symptoms stirred well into some
    months,
the spluttering snowscape stepping toward us.

It is spoon's metal tongue tilling

碗底凉透的白粒，是一次外出
摇醒它：犹豫以至于昏睡的定音锤。

是脚，是离开的必然，让位于次要。
是天真的纤维，你显现它
只能求助于夜空替你掀开眼睑。

是你的手拧动另一种潮湿，
仿佛将要丢失的躁意
透过门缝，扶正屋内折断的香气。

(2016)

crisp white grains in the bowl, it is an excursion
to shake it awake: tuning fork's hesitant torpor.

It is foot, inevitable departing, a step back into
　　secondary importance.
It is naive fibre, you reveal it
must seek help from the twilight to pry open your
　　eyes.

It is the other kind of wet your fingers twisted,
like a hot-headed moment about to be lost
through a crack in the door, to put right the room's
　　scent which snapped.

(2016)

醒世篇

1

午间，雨暂时停下，
你终于起身，看成堆的盐
在相框内部散开。

风伸出纤手，揉搓着
降落地面的小雪山。
它们的出生证，挂上窗外

那棵新晋的绿色三叉戟，
夏天的第一只脚
在波尔卡的瓶颈中踮起新的曲度。

Waking the World Chapter

1

Noon, the rain stops for a moment,
you finally get up, see the piled salt
in the picture frame scatter.

The wind stretches its slight hand to brush
the small mound of snow that fell to the earth.
Certificates of birth, hung outside the window

that green trident upstart,
the first foot of summer
tiptoes a new tune from the polka bottleneck.

2

你弯曲的身体,在睡眠中
微肿,像牙痛患者契诃夫的刀
在咬准案板的一刻,
让隔夜的神经愈加铆紧。

随手拈来樱桃,就着晚间的气味
你乳尖般的红痘半熟。

但一撮盐在你踝边聚齐,
环形的影子包裹着
比晚妆更早下垂的那只手。

3

看见一支笔,削去了
命运彩票的直角,但它背后的字
你刮不透。相片里更深的眼睛

2

Sleeping zigzagged your body
swells slightly, like the knife of Chekhov with
    toothache
in the moment it bites down on the board,
hauls tighter the nerves that traverse the night.

Pick up a cherry, your nipplish zit half-ripens
along with the scent of late evening.

But a pinch of salt collects by your ankle,
the looped shadow parcels
the hand that ducked out before the night's make-
    up was done.

3

See a pen, scratch off a corner
of the scratchcard of fate, though the word on the
    back

后退着，探出一把镊子。

伸向何处？你在更暗的地方
轻吼。"昨日的邮差"，
当你谈论它，滚在水洼里的低音
能否唤醒一间新的卧室。

而腐朽赐你，也刚刚抹平的雨雾。
它的巨眼从铡刀上返照，
修剪完花枝，像事后的你
与你并排躺在一起。

(2016)

can't be scraped away. The deeper eyes in the photo
are retreating, with tweezers held forth.

Stretching where ? You are in a darker place
howling soft. "The courier of yesterday":
when you speak of this, the bass rumbling in puddles
whether or not it can rouse a new bedroom.

Yet decay is conferred unto you, and has just wiped
    flat the mist.
Its huge eyes scan the shears' blades,
pruning the stems, like you after the act
and you lying shoulder to shoulder.

(2016) (tr. by Stephen Nashef)

甜河　Tian He

甜河 (1992–),诗人,生于安徽潜山,现就读于巴黎高等艺术研究院。其作品曾获北京大学未名诗歌奖、复旦大学光华诗歌奖、南京大学重唱诗歌奖。

Tian He, Chinese poet, born in 1992 at Qianshan, Anhui Province, currently lives in Paris, studying at Institut d'Etudes Supérieures des Arts. She has been awarded the Wei-Ming Poetry Prize from the Peking University, the Guang-Hua Poetry Prize from the Fudan University and Chong-Chang Poetry Prize from the Nanjing University.

雨地

沿着东海岸,太平洋递来伶仃的雨,
触碰岛屿锯齿般的边陲,尾随虚弱的
地平线晃动。边走边找蜷缩的卵石。
遍地凹凸不平,布满沙砾。礁石怏怏
而发暗,没有阳光,热情匮乏的海域
带来一些阴沉的满足。我走进雨地越来越
窄小的入口:"这冬季寒流中的女猎手。"
泥泞中季节倒错,堆叠起波浪的长音,
反反复复,冲刷这片憔悴的黑色海岸,

In the Rain

Along the East Sea shore, the Pacific brings a paltry rain,
to touch the craggy edges of the isle, shudders in pursuit
of the frail horizon, rummaging curled up pebbles as it goes.
Everywhere the land is rugged, full of grit, the reef run-
    down;
it darkens, has no sunlight, a seaside lacking warmth,
a little gratifying grim in tow. I walk into the rain's
constricting entrance: "This winter cold front huntress."
The season slips up in the mud, piling up the waves' long
    vowels,
crashing over and over, rinsing the brittle blackness of the
    shore.

缓解忧郁的热病。高耸的棕榈稀疏地
排列，树叶因空气的湿度而凝重。
远处深潜着鲸群，如蛰居的病态沉积，
捕捉阵雨的讯息。海边垂钓的人
小心走入愈来愈大，灰白的风浪。
波涛翻卷着造势，对峙根深蒂固的引力。
黄昏的余光之中，宁静成倍滋长。
在渐暗的海堤上行走，会有美妙的盐
曲折飘入我的喉咙。暮雨提着灯笼返航，
越过北回归线，身体的潮汐被拨至
顶点。"突如其来，你变得小而轻"。
模糊的风暴杳杳而来，耐心垂询
温情的密电，缓慢铺开绵厚的宽掌，
被一闪而过的快乐擦伤。爱人的性
是远在中央的黑暗，夏天尚未到来。
细细的海风，像握紧了迟钝的发辫
我一生都不想松开。

It softens gloom, that tropical disease. The towering palms are sparsely
lined, their leaves slouch heavy from the wetted air.
Sunk in the distance hide a school of whales, the precipitate of some concealed disease,
they snatch at news within the rain while seaside fishers
are careful as they wade out through the growing grey-white chop.
The waves fold as they build in force, that transverse deep-seated pull.
In what light's left of dusk the quiet grows and multiplies.
To walk by the sea wall getting dark will mean exquisite salts
floating tangled paths into my throat. The night-rain holding torch aloft returns ashore
across the Tropic of Cancer, my body's tide set to its
peak. "And just like that you're small and light."
A blurred wind rises from the dim, calmly enquires
as to the coded traffic of human warmth, its silk-thick palm unfolding slowly
is scraped sore by a fleeting dash of joy. The sex of lovers
is the darkness in that distant centre, summer has not yet arrived.
The fine sea-wind, like dopey pigtails held tight in a fist,
I never want the grip released.

真实 | # Real

春天还不真实。登楼
翠色趋于繁忙。凉夜如铁，
花的舌头干燥，火热
（"好德如好色"）
花的舌头还很浅。

甜蜜的余唾还不真实。
嬉闹，抱紧我的麒麟臂
你踮脚为虚空掌灯。待
夕光昏照，我苦味的孔雀
涉险，为我洗心革面。

猜一猜，你细心如兰
如何按捺兵戈之气？
口渴还不够真实。
猜一猜，你细雨的气质

Spring isn't quite real. Up the stairs
the greens tend into bustle. The night cold like
   iron,
flower's tongue dry, hot
（"drawn to the grand as to the carnal"）
flower's tongue slight still.

The spare drivel of honey isn't quite real.
High jinks, gripped to my kylin shoulders
up on your toes to hold a light to the void. Awaiting
the gloaming, my acrid peacock
braves it for me to wipe clean the slate.

Try to figure it out. Your concern fine like orchids
how can the force of the battle be held in check?
Thirst isn't quite real enough.
Try to figure it out. Your mood like fine rain
amassing each day, how can you be drawn to the

与日俱增，如何好客？

那斗室里翘起的，覆弄
眉眼还是飞檐？剩余你
出神，也是原地空转。
花，持续的上升者，学习
空空如也的风姿。

    guest？
Does what rises in our poky room smother
the amorous glance or the roof's lip？The you that
    remains
departs from yourself, left running on empty.
Flower, the persistent ascender, studies
vacancy's poise.

(tr. by Stephen Nashef)

薡弦　Su Xian

薡弦（1993—），诗人，兼事文学批评，现就读于复旦大学中文系。曾获飞地诗歌奖・青年诗人奖、《星星》诗刊年度大学生诗人奖、北京大学未名诗歌奖等。

Su Xian, Chinese poet and critic, was born in 1993, currently majoring at modern & contemporary Chinese literature at the Fudan University. He was awarded the *Enclave* Poetry Prize for Young Poets, the Annual Young Poet Prize by *Star Poetry Journal* and Weiming Poetry Prize from the Peking University.

宿舍

Dormitory

渐渐地，我怀疑宿舍是一只狡黠的貔貅，
在我入睡后，啃噬过期的财经杂志。
收缴钥匙、钢镚、交通卡，还有抄满德语的
便笺纸，不规则动词变化着书堆的形态，
稍有动静，就为生活制造一场雪崩。
甚至抽屉深处，几首未竟之作也被无情地吞咽，
徒留新我向旧我索要，逝去的记忆和灵感。
他始终不动声色，表现得足够内敛，
几乎超越了内外，醉心于曼妙的拓扑学。

Little by little, I suspect there is a cunning Pixiu in my
dormitory after I fall asleep; he might bite the old financial
magazines, take over keys, coins, transportation cards and
sticky notes with German conjugation. Irregular verbs
transform the shape of the books & with the slightest action
　　createan avalanche of life.
Even several unfinished works hidden in the drawers are
　　also swallowed by him
Leaving the new me making demands of the old me for
　　access to the lost memories and inspiration.
He always stays calm, and behaves introvertedly,
almost exceeding the distinction between inside
　　and outside & obsessing in his graceful topology.
Sometimes, in his stomach, the lamp and I are staring
at each other: Twenty watts of the tears are gastric acid
　　digesting the superfluous sorrow.

有时，我在他腹中，与台灯久久对视，

二十瓦的眼泪如胃酸，消化着悲伤的赘物。

更多时候，我只是他神经网络里的

一抹乌云，一个程序设计上的小小错误，

来不及脱身，就被"母体"强劲地扫除。

种种迹象表明，他的成长意味着逐步收缩，

在床头、桌脚，在两扇柜门之间

我曾读懂家具的不愿妥协，像昨夜打翻的

保温瓶，用满地碎银，控诉时空的逼仄。

我则暗暗惊叹彼此相似之处，同样突兀，

同样尴尬，同样"热衷于责任而毫无办法"①

这向我压迫而来的四壁，耗尽了光阴的弹性。

终有一日，我会融入铁屋的呼吸，像所有

曾经呐喊的房客那样，等待新生推门进来。

---

①出自马雁《北京城》。

But most of the time, I am just a bush of dark clouds
& a system design error in his nerve's networks
I am deep cleaned by the 'matrix' before escaping
From all the indications, his growth means gradual shrinkage.
Among the bedside table's legs and the two cabinet doors,
I recognize the stubbornness of the furniture, like the
vacuum flask that was broken last night, accusing its silver fragments on floor.
I am amazed we are similarly abrupt, similarly embarrassed
similarly "crazy about responsibilities but have nowhere to go." ①
These walls oppress me, have exhausted the elasticity of time
One day, I will also be integrated into this iron house's
breath, like all the previous yelling tenants, waiting for the
freshman to push open the door and come in.

---

① A line quoted from Ma Yan's poem "Beijing City".

为背景乐中的修草工而作

1

走近我，还在半睡半醒间，
趁热浪涌上聒噪的工地前，
半透明的海水逐渐膨胀，起伏。
从隐喻的堤岸，推至论证要点，
裁去了彼此学院生活的花边，
割草机的雄辩源自他强劲的心力，
使新城迅速区别于旧租界。
鸽子，这闪电的身手，逾越了
藩篱，在错落的单杠上停顿，
投下几粒阴影，全是自然的碎屑。
而他，正如一根晷针，站进
盛夏的荣光，作为对深浅更谨慎的
切割——时间开始了变化。

The Gardener in the Soundtrack

1

walks close to me while I am still half asleep,
translucent seawater slowly swells and fluctuates
before the hot wave reaches the clamorous construction
   site.
From the embankment of metaphors to the kernel
of an argument, he cuts off the lace of our academic
life the eloquence of the grass cutter originates from its
strong mindforce rapidly distinguishing the new city
   from the old concession.
In a flash of lighting, a pigeon is surmounting the fence,
stops by the uneven horizontal bars
casting grains of shadow, all fragments of nature;
but he, just as the hand of a sundial, stands into
the glory of midsummer, as a more prudent craving
of the gradation – Time begins to change.

2

走近我，就在发痒的耳道口，

割草机的呓语和蝉鸣相互较劲，

神秘得像是意外截获的脑电波。

草尖因此掉落，在衣领外

围成一圈防风林，琐碎之物

反倒更具体，填补我一贯的大意。

并非不能，重温机械的残梦，

反刍草籽、光斑，和伪装一位

园丁的心情。当他沉重的脚踵

当真绕过灌木的寸头，在我

颈椎上停顿，快感，有如惊悸的

栗鼠，闯入街角潜意识的花房，

不过刹那——他已改变了旧我。

2

walks close to me right at the entrance of the ear canal with grass-cutter's somniloquence against cicada chirping, mysterious as a brainwave caught unexpectedly.
The tips of the grass begin to fall, outside of the collar constructing a windbreak circle; Fragments are instead more concrete, remedying my usual carelessness.
It's not that I can't to go over the remanent dream of machine & ruminate on the grass seed, facula and the mood of pretending to be a gardener.
When his heavy steps bypass bush's buzz cut & pause on my neck, the sense of pleasure is a terrified chestnut mouse, intruding on the subconscious greenhouse in the street corner for only a second – He already changed the old me.

(tr. by Jiaoyang Li & Cassandra Atherton)

泉子 Quan Zi

泉子 (1973–)，浙江淳安人，现居杭州。著有诗集《雨夜的写作》《与一只鸟分享的时辰》《秘密规则的执行者》《杂事诗》《湖山集》等。

Quan Zi, born in 1973 at Chun'an, Zhejiang province, now lives at Hangzhou. He is the author of several poetry collections including *Writing in a Rainy Night*, *A Moment Shared with A Bird*, *The Implementer of Secret Rules*, *Miscellaneous Poems* and *A Book of Lake and Hills*.

我宁愿看到的是一堆灰烬

这个七十来斤仿佛装着枯枝的皮袋子
是那个魁伟的一百六十斤的身体的延续吗
这个嘴角上挂满口水，甚至无法分辨自己的名
　字的人
是那个睿智、果断的中年人的延续吗
这个任由女医生扒光他的裤子
在他的生殖器上更换导尿管而面无表情的人
（哦，他那未成年，但已出落得亭亭玉立的女儿

I'd Rather See a Pile of Ashes

Is this body, eighty-some pound leather bag stuffed
　with dead branches,
the continuation of that once robust man of 170
　pounds?
Is this man, drooling from the corners of his mouth
　so much that he is unable to speak his own name,
the continuation of that once witty and decisive
　middle-aged man?
Is this slack-faced man who allowed the doctor to

正站在他的对面）

是那个视尊严如生命的男人的延续吗

不，我宁愿相信这是两个毫不相干的部分

我宁愿看到的是一堆灰烬

甚至，我宁愿看到的是一个被车轮碾成的肉团

是的，我依然相信生命短暂，而灵魂不死

那么，此刻他的灵魂一定在俯视他曾经

甚至在此刻依然归在他名下的丑陋的肉身

他是否有着与我相同的愤怒与绝望

或者，他正在尝试着去理解

这里有着神的不为我们所知的苦心

(2005)

---

strip off his pants

and insert a catheter into his penis

(Oh, with his slender adolescent daughter growing

into her beauty standing close)

the man who would guard his honor like life

itself?

No. I'd rather believe it two lives unrelated.

I'd rather see a pile of ashes

or even a lump of flesh crushed by wheels.

Yes, I believe that life fleets away yet the soul always

lasts

and now the lasting soul of his must be inspecting

from high above this ugly body which was and even

is attached to his name.

Does he share this same anger and despair with

me?

Or perhaps he is trying to comprehend

the unknown pains God takes with us.

(2005)

所以我爱你

这是一个佘祥林的国度，但是我爱你；
这是一个魏则西的国度，但是我爱你；
这是一个雷阳的国度，但是我爱你；
这依然是老庄、孔孟的国度，
所以我爱你；
这依然是屈原、李白、杜甫与东坡居士的国度，
所以我爱你，
这依然是周敦颐、朱熹、王阳明的国度，
所以我爱你，
这依然是我的父亲，一退休乡村教师胡星贵，
与我的母亲，淳朴而善良的农村妇女项彩凤，
是依然盛放着他们全部的悲与喜的国度，
所以我爱你！

(2016)

So I Love You

So it's the land of wrongly imprisoned people like She Xianglin, yet I love you;
So it's the land of victims of online medical scams like Wei Zexi, yet I love you;
So it's the land of victims of police brutality like Lei Yang, yet I love you; So I love you,
for it's also the land of masters like Zhuangtzi, Confucius and Mencius;
So I love you,
for it's also the land of poets like Qu Yuan, Li Bai, Du Fu and Su Shi;
So I love you,
for it's also the land of my philosophers like Zhou Dunyi, Zhu Xi and Wang Yangming;
So I love you,
for it's also the land of my father Hu Xinggui--a retired old country teacher;
So I love you,
for it's also the land of my mother Xiang Yufeng--a kind and modest country woman.
And it's the land that enshrined all their joys and sorrows,
so I love you.

(2016) (tr. by Wang Shali & David Perry)

贾勤 Jia Qin

贾勤（1980- ），诗人，生于延安，2000 年开始跨文体写作，中国美术学院视觉中国研究院特约研究员。
Jia Qin, Chinese poet, born in 1980 at Yan'an, initiated his inter-textuality writing in 2000, now serving as a senior research fellow at the Chinese Institute for Visual Studies in China Academy of Art.

飞

飞上枝头的鸽子并没有给我带来相应的欢喜
大雨迷漫的早晨使昨夜的休息变得扑朔迷离
而那些雾仿佛多疑的间谍它们不同于霞与露
它们不同不是因为要展示自己或者使我观察

它们带着更多的消息消失在昼夜轮转的时刻
它们没有坐骑没有随从仿佛年轻旅人的奔走
但是伴随着巨响携带着风雷创造寂寞的意境
人类在仰望与选择中看清并等待着命定之神

Fly

Pigeons o'er the branches haven't brought me
　　corresponding pleasure,
Mornings in the rain make last night's rest
　　confusingly expire.
O the fog is a distrustful spy, differ from dew and
　　clouds,
'Tis not for display, nor is it for my observation.

They disappeared with more information as the day
　　turned around.
They have no steeds or followers, like hasty young

我只能一意孤行在果实累累的时候任其坠落
无从限制的深情在泪水中凝结成为智慧之源
有一天某人手抚朱弦秘密追随转移中的真理

从容觉醒的歌者甚至认为他的歌唱可以稍息
整体的文明破碎之后还有什么东西继续扩散
提问者陷入了巨大的沉思他的心却平静如水

travelers.
But they create loneliness with wind and thunder
Look up and choose, see and wait for a destined
    order.

I can only go on my own and let the fruit fall when it
    is full.
Boundless affection condenses into wisdom in tears.
One day a hand touched the string secretly to follow
    the truth in transit.

The singer awakened with ease even thinks his
    singing can be at ease.
What will continue to spread after the collapse of
    entire civilization.
The questioner is deep in thought but his heart is still
    as water.

爱

爱着月亮在高空设下的悬梯

爱着自然的露水垂落在黎明破晓的时刻那是
时间起始白昼降临的预兆而万物在此前确
已得到滋养

爱着无垠之水它与生命的关系仿佛是天经地义
而我却看出了端倪在大水中获得永生的冲
动暂时忘记了它的流逝此时明亮之水借鉴
包举遍彻了心意

爱着单纯的火在时间中吞吐它的呼吸产生了
大量气体它经过的地方不可能毫无痕迹然
后它遁藏于石头的核心即使一再邀请才偶
尔作答它坚持更高的原则

爱着创造中的天地它弘穆坚实忍受一切任你
生物的繁衍任你无机物的尘埃舞动任你内
心的踊跃引发火山作瞬间的喜悦之震同时自
由旋转于苍穹

Love

In love with the moon's hanging ladder

In love with the dew that falls at the dawn of daybreak a
sign of time beginning and of the coming of day and of
all things that were nourished before

In love with the boundless water's relationship with life
which seems natural and I see an impulse to live forever
in the great water and I forget its passage for a while and
the bright water envelopes and penetrates my mind

In love with the pure fire which swallows its breath and
makes a lot of fumes and can't go anywhere without a
trace but hides in the core of the stone responding only
occasionally to repeated summons and adhering to a
higher principle

In love with the world's creation which is sumptuous and
concrete enduring the multiplication of all creatures,
the dancing of inorganic dust the instant of rapture
from the inner volcano rotating freely in the firmament

In love with the world civilization flying through war and
death, extending the drift or meaning of the universe

爱着天下的文明在战火与死亡中飞动引申万物
　　创造了和平的象征此种手法在期待中一时难
　　以领会目睹它的人类仿佛若有所思但是面对
　　繁复的物象他们不可能直接承诺
爱着尘世间的足音那踩踏泥土的声响包含了亲
　　人们沉默的辛苦他们劳作不单单是为了自己
　　看呵游戏中的儿童将要告别童年
爱着不变的属于诗人的表达毫无疑问地宣布了
　　同类的消息那种神话与传说中塑造的生存以
　　及惯用的表情
爱着辉煌的殿宇无论何种信仰我们都已拜受无
　　形中抵达的秘境或者竟如秋日般明朗也许更
　　像春天的枝条夏季的果实冬日的根须
爱着形容肯定一切促进一切此种形容早已引起
　　了我的关注

and creating a symbol of peace so difficult to
　　understand that humans witnessing it try to think
　　or promise but cannot when they directly face its
　　complicated images and objects
In love with the footsteps in the world of dust which
　　contain the silent painstaking traces of loved ones who
　　work not only for themselves but for the children look
　　they are playing games saying goodbye to their
　　childhood
In love with the unchanging expression of the poet who
　　without fail presents the same kind of material that is
　　the myth and the legend of survival and so on
　　according to customary expression
In love with the brilliant palace we arrive at virtually
　　no matter what we believe in which may be serene
　　as sunshine in autumn or branches in spring fruits in
　　summer or roots in winter
In love with description with affirmation of appearance
　　that attracts my attention, prompts and promotes this
　　description

(tr. by Song Zhe & Amelia Dale)

茱萸 Zhu Yu

茱萸（1987– ），本名朱钦运，江西赣州人，诗人，青年批评家，哲学博士。出版诗文集多种，现供职于苏州大学文学院。
Zhu Yu, original name Zhu Qinyun, was a native of Ganzhou, Jiangxi Province. Both a post-80s poet and a critic with a PhD, he is the author of several poetry collections. Now he teaches at College of Liberal Arts, Soochow University (Suzhou).

梨花或者绝句 / Pear Blossoms or Quatrains

十指交缠，节候开始呼吸
惊艳之名从花谱间簌簌站起
那花瓣穿过一首旧诗的颈联
朝闪烁在指间的绿色走去
风那么大，只带来飞鸟的羽毛

我喜欢那些转瞬即逝的事物
譬如鸟羽，或者梨花。它们
变成水，兼具飞翔及流淌的特质

with fingers entwined, the seasons begin to breath
from the index of flowers startling names rustle up to their feet
a petal passes through an old poem's third line
and heads to the green that glimmers between fingers
a wind so great it brought but birds' feathers

I like things which pass with a flicker,
like pear blossoms or feathers, they become water,
have something both of drift and of flight
or speaking a strong local accent of the bloom and the wilt
with someone just passing through, they move forth

或操着浓重的地方口音，和驻足者
谈及的盛开与凋零，都在暗地进行

我知道我们之间的谈话很轻
一万首绝句摔落地面的声音
偕同梨花吐露的颜色与消息
轻易地将我们的谈话擦去：它涉及
一切柔软事物的内心和外貌

undercover

I know that our conversation is slight
the sound of a thousand quatrains as they drop to the floor
attends the colour and message the pear blossoms reveal
brushing soft past the words we exchange:
they concern all pliable things, both interior and carriage

沈复：浮槎遗事

谁看见水的花朵那要命的宏大之数
在水的地板上移动？
　　　　　——史蒂文斯《充满云的海面》

临海的山是大陆伸出的手指，它一旦
用造化的臂力抓回浅滩，我们就要
彼此成为孤独的岛屿。何况诗的失忆
至多算是惭愧地治疗，从这里的出走
只接近过梦幻余生那焦躁的边缘——

最艰难的一步是从疲惫中醒来，哀愁
成为命数的燃料，而你所记录的浮生
并不见得比航海日志更接近天地本然。
一艘海船如今稳稳地泊在全面失守的
中年，远方的景色比起室内、园中或
旅途的风尘，被赋予了更高的乐趣。
散文决定了航向。随着十九世纪远去，
它们差点湮没于集市的冷摊，而作者

Shen Fu: Old Stories of a Raft Which Drifts

Who saw the mortal massives of the blooms
Of water moving on the water–floor?
　　　　　—Wallace Stevens "Sea Surface Full of Clouds"

Once the sea-peering mountain, the land's pointed finger,
with forger's brawn hooked back in the shoals, we became
each other's lonely islands. And yet, a poem's compulsion
to forget is at most a means for salving shame; our flight from
here has only neared the edgy brink, our dreams ahead—

The hardest step is waking from unwilled fatigue, grief grows
fate's fuel, and what you wrote of life which drifts
seems no closer to the stuff of things than shipmen's logs.
A skiff now floats securely moored in middle age,
the subsiding mass. The distant scene, more than time
in cabins, gardens or mid-voyage, is fitted with a higher joy.

Prose plots the course. As the 1800s took its leave your works
were nearly lost to nameless piles in quiet stalls. Yet
 'fore casting off, all writers have to meet the storms

出海前正遭遇着来自日常生活的风暴；
另一些丢失的手札上据说还存有墨色
正在枯萎，证明你曾涉足偏远的海国，
并研习过养生术以便适应未来的生活。

有人将这样的历险视为闲情，似乎
远比从山腰朝南方海域眺望要安全。

新的危机是来自同代人的艳羡，他们
失陷于激动人心的客套与虚伪的表情。
果肉吞着核，水饺藏着馅，宴会的细节
能再次包裹我们的脆弱，使海边轻声
交谈的人只醉心于你隐约透露的逸闻②

of life ashore. It's said another's jottings still harbour ink:
rotting proof you travelled seas to far-off states
and pursued a science of health for life ahead.

Some take these exploits for a lighter pleasure, it seems far
  safer
than to gaze out from a ridge into the southward sea.

The crisis now is what our peers resent. They lose
themselves to false expressions, fired-up cliché. The fruit
engulfs the stone, the dumpling its filling, and the feast
wraps our frailer parts in its minutiae, drunken those who
  softly
talk at ocean's edge, on your tales and their discreet
  reveal.

(tr. by Stephen Nashef)

张尔　Zhang Er

张尔（1976–），诗人，深圳《飞地》主编。著有诗集《乌有栈》《壮游图》等。
Zhang Er, Chinese poet, born in 1976, now serves as the Chief Editor of *Enclave* based in Shenzhen, publishing several poetry collections including *Grand Tour Map* and *Nowhere Inn*.

布吉河小夜曲

黄昏，河道阻隔着灰雨和铁路
电线收拢密集的白昼，云层渐黯
直至被无边的沉寂囫囵吞咽
仿佛身陷另一座伪大陆

有人在对岸冥想、慢跑
保持着孤立者羞耻的尺度
然后，是更为长久地斡旋
像夜色之下，一匹失踪的金毛斜翘起后足

Buji River Serenade

Sunset, gray rain and railroad tracks blockaded by the river
power lines gather concentrated daylight, clouds grow dim
yill they are swallowed by boundless silence
as if they had sunken into a counterfeit continent

Someone meditates while jogging on the other side
maintaining the standard for an outsider's sense of shame
afterwards, an even longer negotiation
like a golden retriever that has gone missing lifting his hind leg
　　under the night sky
A few rainbow Mobikes drive out of the abandoned lumber
　　processing plant
drawing near from a distance, carrying on their backs a docile
　　economy on the wing

几辆彩虹摩拜,驶出废弃的木柴加工厂
由远及近,驮起翩翩顺从的经济
雨后河水加速湍急
徒留共享的节奏和化学

捕鱼客从怀中掏出探照灯,果断地瞄准
桥拱下,那受惊的白鹭瞬间划出
一道紧急抛物线
他怀孕的妻子倚身栅栏,俯视

鱼篓的盛宴,赤脚孩童
手举染毒的病鱼争相合影
三角岛上,情人们趁黑偷吻
肢体仓促的忸怩,形似蹩脚的探戈

夜幕污浊而令人警醒
雨滴洗濯脱钙的城市与楼群
绿皮火车口衔大地暴露的铁轨
隆隆噪音犁开一曲隐匿的休止符

after the rain the torrent in the river gains speed
leaving behind a shared rhythm and chemistry in vain

A fisherman takes out a search light from his vest and aims
    resolutely
Under the arch bridge, a startled white heron draws in an
    instant a parabolic arc of urgency in the sky
His pregnant wife leans on the railing and gazes down

at the feast in the fish basket; barefooted children
holding toxic, sick fish in their hands vie to take pictures
On the triangular island, lovers steal kisses in the dark
The hurried tangling of limbs looks like a graceless Tango

The night curtain is filthy and alarming
Raindrops wash the calcium-deficient city and its clustered
    buildings
A green-coated train touches the track exposed by earth
its rumbling ploughs open a tune of hidden rests

(2017) (tr. by Michelle Yeh)

交通协奏曲

昼夜冷暖,声波挑动星辰协奏
大地的地毯横陈轻工业,收拢你
赤脚踩踏木楼的区区片刻与苦心
橡胶撩街道,齿轮戏轴承

灰烬纵情弹跳,身手之快如琴键闪屏
霓虹,汇入涌动的洪流
摇曳的尾影,丈量一尺微微轻喜剧
那微型老爷车,迟钝地驶出马萨诸塞州

人货皮卡斜拖一架宇宙帆船
度白人繁复的长假,冒黑烟喷嚏如卷发
你旋转下楼,拣起越洋联邦快递
层叠的书卷,《诗经》般
砌成一座十字架。萨莫维尔 T 字街口
垃圾装卸车缓缓吞吐雷雨的警笛

Traffic Concerto

Night and day of daily life, sound waves set off a starry
    accompaniment
the earth's spread-eagle carpet of industry gathers you in
barefoot and trampling the wooden buildings' brief trifling
efforts rubber-teased streets, gear-played ball bearings

Ashes indulge in bouncing, skillful as keystrokes flashing on a
screen neon gathers in a torrent
flickering shadows measure a few inches of comedy
a toy vintage car slowly starts up in Massachusetts

Pickups with goods and people pull the sailboat of the universe
on a Westerner's complex vacation, I blow black smoke like
curls of hairyou spin downstairs, pick up some international
    mail
piles of books, like the Book of Songs
piling up like a crucifix. At an intersection in Somerville
a garbage truck slowly spits out its thundering sirens

(tr. by Eleanor Goodman)

黄礼孩 Huang Lihai

黄礼孩，70后诗人，生于海南徐闻，现居广州。出版诗集《我对命运所知甚少》《给飞鸟喂食彩虹》（英文版）《谁跑得比闪电还快》（波兰文版）等。1999年创办《诗歌与人》，2005年设立"诗歌与人·国际诗人奖"。

Huang Lihai, post-70s poet, born in Xuwen, Hainan Province, now lives in Guangzhou. He is the author of several poetry collections including *I Know Little about Life*, *Feed Birds Rainbows* (English Edition) and *Who can Outrun the Lightning?* (Polish Edition). He established the poetry magazines *Poetry & People* in 1999, and "Poetry & People Poet Prize".

我爱它的沉默无名 / I Love Its Silence and Obscurity

夜气，星宿在上升
密纹唱片发出柔和之声
年轻的传说点亮了爱
清冷地悬在蜘蛛网上
那些听着自己回音的昆虫
身上已经覆盖了发亮的露珠

蓝条纹的丘陵群鸟一样穿过
少女起伏的秀发

Stars rise together
Gentle music hovers over a record's microgrooves
Young legend brightens love
Insects indulge in their own echoes
Suspended coldly on spider web and
Find themselves covered with shining dews

Blue stripped hills pass like flocks of birds
Or a girl's beautiful hair waving

游弋的线条是时光的窃贼

仿佛大海深处水草的梦境

缓慢地沉入，菠萝地里

我的凝念由此而生

这无边缄默的菠萝的海

在它尚未被命名之前

我保存着这份空缺

只爱它的沉默无名

(2017)

Cruising lines are stealing and hiding time

Like dreams of seaweed deep down the ocean

Slowly sinking into the pineapple fields

Thus my suspicion rises

From the boundless pineapple fields in silence

Long before it got its name

I keep this vacancy

As I love its silence and obscurity

(2017)

伤口也在散发出光芒

生活的清单喋喋不休

阅读之书翻向稍纵即逝的光

过去与未来在指间腾挪

你躺在床上看书，文字瞬间转向

如无系之舟划向陌生的海域

至性的波浪，此起彼伏

生活遗忘的部分，心在提醒

读一本新诗集，它动荡，寂静

偶尔有温柔射出

裂锦般的声音释放着什么

你翻阅着半隐半现的暗物质

意外的纸片划破了手指

你端详细小的伤口

发现它也在散发出什么

(2017)

The Wound Is Sending Forth Glory

Life's list is chattering on and on
While the book you are reading is turning into
    transient light
Past and future converge between fingers
Lying in bed you are reading, words swerve
Like an untied boat sailing into unknown waters
As one wave falls another rises

Your heart is reminding you of the forgotten part
    of your life,
You start to read a new collection of poems and it
    is both turbulent and tranquil
At times it lets out gentleness
But sounds like brocade ripping
You go through dark matter that is half obscure
    half distinct
One page accidentally cuts your finger
Scrutinizing the tiny wound
You find it is also radiating something

(2017)(tr. by Yujun Yang & Cassandra Atherton)

冯娜　Feng Na

冯娜（1985-），诗人，生于云南丽江，白族，现任职于中山大学。著有《无数灯火选中的夜》《寻鹤》《一个季节的西藏》等诗文集多部。

Feng Na, Chinese poet of *Bai* minority, born in 1985, in Lijiang, Yunnan Province. She works in Sun Yat-sen University, and is an author of several poetry collections including *A Night Filled with Lights*, *Searching for Cranes*, and *Tibet of One Season*.

出生地

人们总向我提起我的出生地

一个高寒的、山茶花和松林一样多的藏区

它教给我的藏语，我已经忘记

它教给我的高音，至今我还没有唱出

那音色，像坚实的松果一直埋在某处

夏天有麂子

冬天有火塘

当地人狩猎、采蜜、种植耐寒的苦荞

火葬，是我最熟悉的丧礼

Birthplace

People always bring up my birthplace,

a cold Yunannese place with camellias and pines.

It taught me Tibetan, and I forgot.

It taught me a tenor; I haven't sung

That register is a hard pine nut, hidden somewhere.

There are Muntjacs in the summer

and fire pits in winter.

The locals hunt, harvest honey, plant buckwheat

because it's hardy. Pyres are familiar:

we don't ask about the private life of death

我们不过问死神家里的事
也不过问星子落进深坞的事

他们教会我一些技艺
是为了让我终生不去使用它们
我离开他们
是为了不让他们先离开我
他们还说,人应像火焰一样去爱
是为了灰烬不必复燃

or ask comets striking ruts in the earth.

They taught me certain arts
so that I might never use them.
I left them
so they wouldn't leave me first.
They said that loving should be like fire
so that ashes needn't need to burst into life.

回声

——致卡伦·布里克森

你到达的地方,东南方向

长眠着一位我喜欢的作家

我测算过那些经度和纬度网罗的春天

她的灵魂干渴

却再也不需要更多的传记

在那里,你、我,和她一样

可以从任何自然的事物中获得完整的形体

一个傍晚,你要雕塑我的嘴唇

一座塔楼远离墓园

你让她从我喷泉般的语调中复活

咖啡树林、受伤的狮子、三支来复枪……

文稿在烛火中燃尽

谁继承了这痛苦而热情的天赋

Echo

—For Karen Blixen

Where you're going, to the southeast

a writer I like is buried

I have measured along spring's latitudes

her spirit is parched

but the biographies have said enough

There you and I, and she alike

can see through seem, to the bones of things

One evening, you want to carve my mouth

a tower bordering a graveyard

you'd like me to describe her

The trees are coffee colored, the lions wounded

the rifles that did it over there…

A manuscript burns above the candle

who inherits the gift, enkindled, impassioned?

我又一次在空中目睹那动荡之地

一动不动的容颜

她走过漫长的峡谷，和你一样

肉体像日光一样工作

去辨识每一种香料根茎、花朵、树皮的差异

在这里，死亡满足了所有人的幻象

在这里，富有和贫穷是等值的

她在我头顶举起树荫

呵，我从来不曾相信墓志铭中的谎言

雨水却盛满中国南部的咸味

"不，不要再开口祈祷"

你说，美用不着石碑上冷冰冰的纪念

河水的反光，让我有片刻的晕眩

人们那些可怕的念头、过度的怯懦

摇晃着船只

我盯紧水中的光芒

我和她一样，并非是人类中最虔诚的信徒

Viewed from a great height, against the trembling

ground, her motionless face

Like you, she has crossed many canyons

her body is like the sun

and touches each spice, vine, flower, and piece of

bark differently

Here death is satisfying

and poverty and wealth are equidistant

She raises the shadow of a leaf to my head

I have never trusted epitaph's lies

yet the rain is full of southern China's briny

Don't, don't begin to pray

you tell me stone inscriptions are not beautiful

The flashing river light dizzies

those frightening thoughts,

those moments of weakness we have

The boats rock

归巢与启程 中澳当代诗选(中国卷)
Homings and Departures — Selected Poems from Contemporary China and Australia

在你离开的第十一个昼夜

我就发明了一个新的地理坐标:

她穿过市集、修道院、农场、穷人的窗台

在悬崖边上站了一会儿

扭头对我说出了那个词——

and the river's light dazes

Like her, I am not the most devout disciple

The first day after you leave

I discover a new latitude

it goes through hamlets, convents, farms, windows

of the poor stops at the edge of a cliff

turns its head and says to me a word—

(tr. by Henry Zhang & Amelia Dale)

柏桦　Bai Hua

柏桦 (1956–)，20 世纪 80 年代"后朦胧"诗歌运动核心人物，现居四川成都，任教于西南交通大学。
Bai Hua is considered a central literary figure of the Post–Misty poetry movement in contemporary China during the 1980s. Currently living in Chengdu, Sichuan Province, he teaches at the Southwest Jiaotong University.

望气的人

望气的人行色匆匆
登高眺远
眼中沉沉的暮霭
长出黄金、几何与宫殿

穷巷西风突变
一个英雄正动身去千里之外
望气的人看到了
他激动的草鞋和布衫

The Air Alchemist

The air alchemist's in a hurry walking
High, looks far out
Of evening mist his eyes
Grow gold geometry and palaces

West wind abruptly took
Thousands of miles beyond a hero
The air alchemist saw
His straw sandals and shirt agitate

更远的山谷浑然
零落的钟声依稀可闻
两个儿童打扫着亭台
望气的人坐对空寂的傍晚

吉祥之云宽大
一个干枯的导师沉默
独自在吐火、炼丹
望气的人看穿了石头里的图案

乡间的日子风调雨顺
菜田一畦，流水一涧
这边青翠未改
望气的人已走上了另一座山巅

(1986)

Further: valley in harmony
Shattered tolls vaguely heard
Two boys sweep the terrace
The air alchemist sat in lonely lateness

Auspicious cloud, vast
Dry-boned master, silent
Solitary work on alchemical fire
The air alchemist saw patterns inside stone

Country life goes on just fine
A field of vegetables, a stream of water
While this side is still green
The air alchemist is atop another mountain

(Late spring, 1986)

一切黑

飞奔的黑空气里
我听到它的喘气
敛翅伪装的黑瓢虫
打完麻药，准备
做一个开颅手术。

藏而不露黑中黑
黑夜黑发黑衣裤
哪种人？所有人！
常常他们想要的
并非他们所需的。

卷上珠帘总不如
嘴唇黑，喉咙黑
口水浪波非眼波
闪电风暴在滚动！

(2018)

Dark Matter

Galloping black air flying

Gasping air hear

A dark ladybird, wing-folded

Etherized, prepared

For its craniotomy

Hide hoods darkly visible:

Black night on black hair on briefs black

What of them ?   All of them!

What they do are not is want

They ask or wish for often

Pare pearl curtain unroll, unveil

Dark lips larynx dark throat though

Alluring waves of saliva desire but eyes

Rolling storm flash rolling break!

(2018)(tr. by Li Fukang & Amelia Dale)

樊星　Fan Xing

樊星，诗人，译者，现为西澳大学人文学院博士候选人。出版中英双语诗集《兔子在午后梦见爱丽丝》（2009）和《词语的南方》（2018）。

Fan Xing, poet, translator, is a PhD candidate in the School of Humanities at the University of Western Australia. She is the author of two bilingual poetry collections: *Lost in the Afternoon* (2009) and *South of Words* (2018).

北京　夏　二〇〇八

平流层

一只饱含激情，遐思

决心北去的候鸟

泅渡日光下无垠的云海

反刍一种同样属于骆驼

与蓝鲸的寂寞

Beijing Summer 2008

stratosphere

filled with passion, thoughts and plans

a giant bird determined to fly north

through the vastness of sunlit clouds

chewing on cud loneliness

of a saddled camel in the desert

of a blue whale on its road

十五楼的酒店房间

夜读

安娜伊斯宁

目光在灼热的

文字间穿梭

隔音玻璃

包围的寂寞

梦，死静

清早，打开窗

放进雨后

一片潮湿的车声

黑鸟

听到翅膀拍打

黑色的翼掠过天空

我尝试用十三种方法看它

hotel room on the fifteenth floor

at first it smelt strange, untrusting

three days later I found

dreams having weighed on the pillow

it flattened, bed clothes

with sweats of several nights

finally smelt a little like me

blackbird

hearing the sound of flapping

dark glimpse

a flicker on bird's wings

I try to find out thirteen ways to look at this

disappearing and reappearing

in the bush, among trees

and into my mind

weaving word by word

as of an old poem –

消失再现于草丛林间

最后在脑中串成一句古诗

"野鸟入室兮,主人将去"

'a wild bird's entry into a house

foretells the master's departure'

广州假期

1

就这么看见了
在三万九千英尺的高空
地图上横穿不知名岛屿的
一条蓝线

越过赤道
从前的双眼指引你
进出上下班的人潮
找到隧道与隧道
正确的结点

想起一些什么又被新的代替
有些重合、有些偏移

Canton Holiday

1

thirty-nine thousand feet above
a thin blue line runs across
an unknown island on the map

on the other side of the equator
another pair of eyes
lead you through
peak hour crowds

old memories replaced by the new
some names match
their faces, others don't

on a descending escalator
you see people ascending
for the New Year countdown

在上行电梯看

下行电梯上的脸

然后出站倒数过新年

2

她说

在重现历史时

要用陌生化的手法

难道就是说

要用那只流浪猫的

眼光来看？

讲座散场

进地铁站买票

手伸进口袋

摸到两枚

大小不一的

一元硬币

2

she said

when representing history

you need to defamiliarise

does she mean we should see

through the eyes of that stray cat

sliding my hand into my pocket

touched two oneyuan coins

except one slightly bigger

(A response to the Chinese poem by the author)

译者简介 TRANSLATORS BIOS

A.J. CARRUTHERS（卡拉瑟斯）is an Australian-born experimental poet and literary critic. carruthers is a researcher at the Australian Studies Centre, SUIBE, and is author of *Stave Sightings: Notational Experiments in North American Long Poems* (Palgrave 2017) and *AXIS Book 1* (Vagabond 2014), the first volume of an ongoing lifelong long poem, which has been described as a "vast experiment". See also *Opus 16 on Tehching Hsieh* (Gauss PDF 2017) and *The Blazar Axes* (Spacecraft Press 2018).

AJIU（阿九）a professional engineer, is also a Chinese poet and translator living in the Greater Vancouver District, BC, Canada. His first book of poetry, *the Langara Journal,* was published in 2015. A number of other poems have appeared in more than twenty anthologies. He won the PEW prize for translation (2015) in recognition of his earlier translation works. He is also the Chinese translator of *the Complete Poems of Philip Larkin* (2018).

AMELIA DALE（美莲）is a poet, editor, literary critic and researcher at the Australian Research Center in SUIBE, Shanghai. Her most recent book *Constitution* (Inken Publisch), won *Mascara Literary Review*'s Avant-garde award for poetry (2018). Other books include *Grumpy Cat 2 Reads Sanditon Chapter* 2 (gauss pdf) and *Tractosaur* (Troll Thread). Her monograph *The Printed Reader* is forthcoming with Bucknell University Press. She has a PhD from the University of Sydney, is editor-in-chief of SOd Press and on the editorial boards of Rabbit *Poetry Journal* and *Cordite Poetry Review.*

ANDREA LINGENFELTER（凌静怡）published her translations of contemporary Chinese poetry in a number of literary journals and anthologies, including *the Zoland Annual, Hayden's Ferry Review,* and *Circumference.* She is also the translator of the novels Candy, by Mian Mian, and Farewell My Concubine by Lilian Lee (Li Bihua). In 2008 she was awarded a Pen Translation Fund Grant to translate Annie Baobei's 2006 novel, Padma. Her collection of translations of poetry by Zhai Yongming is set for publication by Zephyr Press in 2009. Future projects include Wang Anyi's novel *Qimeng shidai* and a volume of translations of poetry by the Shanghai-based poet Wang Yin.

AUSTIN WOERNER（温侯廷）A Chinese-English literary translator, Austin Woerner has translated two volumes of poetry, *Doubled Shadows: Selected Poetry of Ouyang Jianghe* and *Phoenix,* and edited the English edition of the innovative, bilingual Chinese literary journal *Chutzpah.* He has a BA in East Asian Studies from Yale and an MFA in creative writing from the New School, and he is currently a lecturer at Duke Kunshan University.

BAO HUIYI（包慧怡）, born in Shanghai (1985), PhD. in Old and Middle English Literature (University College Dublin), is assistant professor at the Department of English, Fudan University. She has published two books of poetry, *A Pagan Book of Hours* (2012) and *I Sit on the Edge of the Volcano* (2016); one book of prose, *Annal of the Emerald Isle* (2015); and one book of criticism, *Scriptorium* (2018). She is the translator of twelve books from English to Chinese, including *Complete Poems by Elizabeth Bishop*, *Ariel* by Sylvia Plath, *Good Bones* by Margaret Atwood, and *Immram and Isle: Works of Four Contemporary Irish Poets*. She has authored one monograph in English, *The Pearl-Poet and the Sensorium in Medieval England* (2018), and her monograph in Chinese, *The Art of Middle English Lyrics*, is forthcoming in 2018. She won the China Bookstore Prize (2015), DJS-Poetry East West Award (2013), Literature Ireland Translator's Bursary (2014). She taught at Trinity College Dublin before joining Fudan, and is currently vice director of the China-Australia Creative Writing Centre (CAWC) at Fudan, as well as a member of Shanghai Writers' Association.

CANAAN MORSE（莫楷） is a translator, poet and editor currently based in Boston. He is an original member of *Paper Republic* and co-founder of *Pathlight: New Chinese Writing*, for which he was the first Poetry Editor. His translations and book reviews have appeared in several international journals both in print and online, and he was the winner of the 2014 Susan Sontag International Prize for Translation. He holds an M.A. in Classical Chinese Literature from the Chinese Language and Literature Department at Peking University.

CASSANDRA ATHERTON（卡桑德拉·阿瑟顿） is a widely anthologised prose poet and one of Australia's leading experts on prose poetry. She was a visiting scholar in English at Harvard University in 2016 and a visiting fellow at Sophia University, Tokyo, in 2014. Cassandra has published 17 critical and creative books and is the successful recipient of more than fifteen national and international research grants and awards, including a Creative Victoria grant and an Australia Council grant. She has judged poetry awards including the Victorian Premier's Prize for Poetry, the joanne burns award and the Lord Mayor's Prize for Poetry. She is an Associate Professor of Writing and Literature and the current poetry editor of *Westerly* magazine.

DAVID PERRY (戴维·佩里) a poet and translator, published his recent book of poems, *Expat Taxes*, seeking to refract Shanghai's complex identity as both Chinese and a "global" city through the lens of a decade of living in the former French Concession; his current web-based writing project, 16 Lines and Changing emerges from an attempt to write the Shanghai Metro. He is also the author of *Range Finder* (Adventures in Poetry), *Knowledge Follows* (Insurance Editions) and *New Years* (Braincase). He earned his MFA in Literary Translation from the University of Iowa in 1997. Since 2006, he has lived in Shanghai, where he teaches writing at NYU Shanghai.

DENIS MAIR (梅丹理) a poet and translator, is a co-translator of Frontier Taiwan, an anthology of new poetry from Taiwan. His versions of works by Mainland Chinese poets have appeared in *Literary Review*, *Chicago Review*, *Trafika*, *Kritya*, *Melic Review*, *Poetry Sky*, *Point No Point*, *The Temple*, and other journals. His book of poems, *Man Cut in Wood*, was published by Valley Contemporary Press. He has taught Chinese at University of Pennsylvania and Whitman College.

DIANA SHI (史春波), Chinese literary translator, has recent work in the international poetry journals *Circumference*, *La Jornada*, and *Words Without Borders*. In China, her translations have appeared in

Foreign Literature, Chinese-Western Poetry, Razor, and elsewhere. With George O'Connell, she co-edited / co-translated *the Atlanta Review 2008 China Edition*. They are currently assembling an anthology of contemporary Chinese poetry for publication in the U.S.

ELEANOR GOODMAN（顾爱玲） is the author of the poetry collection *Nine Dragon Island* (2016), and the translator of *Something Crosses My Mind: Selected Poems of Wang Xiaoni* (2014), *Iron Moon: An Anthology of Chinese Workers Poetry* (2017), and *The Roots of Wisdom: Poems by Zang Di* (2017). She is a Research Associate at the Harvard University Fairbank Center.

GAO XING（高兴） was born in Jiangsu Province in China and graduated Beijing Foreign Study University in 1987. He is the author of several books of essays and hundreds of poems. He has also translated Milan Kundera, Ivan Klima, Marin Sorescu, Nichita Stanescu, Ana Blandiana, Ismail Kadare, Tomaz Salamun, etc. His poems and essays have been translated into English, Russian, Romanian and many others. Currently he serves as the Editor-in-Chief of *World Literature*, a famous journal in China.

GEORGE O'CONNELL（乔直） American poet, recent Fulbright Professor of Creative Writing and American Literature at Peking University, has won numerous honors in the U.S., including the Pablo Neruda Prize for Poetry and Bellingham Review's 49th Parallel Award. In China, he received the 2007 China Journey Award. With Diana Shi, he co-edited / co-translated *the Atlanta Review 2008 China Edition*. Currently he is a professor of Creative Writing and Literature in S.E. China.

HAI AN（海岸）, pseudonym for Li Dingjun, is a Chinese poet, translator, Associate Professor of English at Fudan University and Associate Chief Editor of *Contemporary Poetry Quarterly* based in Hong Kong. He has published ten books of poetry as the author, translator and editor, including *Selected Poems by Hai An* (2001), *Elegy: A Therapeutic Long Poem* (2012), *When, Like a Running Grave: A Critical Approach to Translating Poems of Dylan Thomas* (2018); *Selected Poems of Dylan Thomas* (2014), *Selected Poems of Samuel Beckett* (2016); *A Centennial Collected Papers on Sino-Occidental Poetry Translation* (2007), *Frontier Tide: Contemporary Chinese Poetry* (2009) and *Homings and Departures——Selected Poems from Contemporary China and Australia* (China Volume, 2018). He was invited to attend several International Poetry Festivals including the 48th Struga International Poetry Evenings in Macedonia in 2009. He is the winner of STA Translation Achievement Award in 2016. [djli@fudan.edu.cn]

HUANG YUNTE（黄运特）is a professor of English at the University of California, Santa Barbara, and Tong Tin Sun Chair Professor of English at Lingnan University, Hong Kong. A Guggenheim fellow, he is the editor of T*HE BIG RED BOOK OF MODERN CHINESE LITERATURE* (Norton, 2016) and the author *of Inseparable* (Liveright, 2018).

LUCAS KLEIN（柯夏智）, PhD Yale, is a father, writer, translator, and assistant professor in the School of Chinese at the University of Hong Kong. His translation *Notes on the Mosquito: Selected Poems of Xi Chuan* won the 2013 Lucien Stryk Prize, and his *October Dedications*, translations of the poetry of Mang Ke, is now available from Zephyr and Chinese University Press. His translations of Tang dynasty poet Li Shangyin are in a volume published by New York Review Books, and his monograph, *The Organization of Distance: Poetry,*

Translation, Chineseness, is published by Brill.

MICHELLE YEH (奚密), born in Taipei, received her Ph.D. in Comparative Literature from the University of Southern California, Los Angeles. Currently she is Professor of Chinese in the Department of East Asian Languages and Cultures, University of California, Davis, as well as Chair of the UC Pacific Rim Research Program. Her major publications include: *Modern Chinese Poetry: Theory and Practice since 1917, Anthology of Modern Chinese Poetry, No Trace of the Gardener: Poems of Yang Mu, Essays on Modern Chinese Poetry, From the Margin: An Alternative Tradition of Modern Chinese Poetry, Frontier Taiwan: An Anthology of Modern Chinese Poetry, Iconography of the Sea: Poems of Derek Walcott*.

SAWAKO NAKAYASU (中保佐和子) was born in Japan and has lived mostly in the US since the age of six. Her books include *Hurry Home Honey* (2009), *Texture Notes* (2009), *Nothing fictional but the accuracy or arrangement (she* (2005), and *So we have been given time Or* (2004). Books of translations include *For the Fighting Spirit of the Walnut* by Takashi Hiraide (2008) which won the 2009 Best Translated Book Award, as well as *Four From Japan* (2006) featuring four contemporary poets. She has received the NEA/JUSFC Fellowship for poetry, and grants from the NEA and PEN for translating Japanese poetry. More information can be found here: [http://www.factorial.org/sn/sn_home.html]

SIMON PATTON (西敏) literary translator, poetry critic and full-time teacher of Chinese language and literature at the University of Queensland. He collaborates closely with mainland Chinese writers to bring their writing to English-language readers. In the past fifteen years, he has been translating Chinese literature, especially contemporary poetry for a new Chinese poetry website launched by the Netherlands-based Poetry International Foundation. [http://china.poetryinternationalweb.org]

STEPHEN NASHEF（施笛闻）was born in Glasgow (Scotland, UK) and lives in Guangzhou where he translates, writes and enjoys literature, particularly poetry. His translations have appeared in *Pathlight* and *Tender Buds: 21st Century Chinese Poems* and he has had an essay published in the US journal *Chinese Literature and Culture*. He was also one of the founding editors of the UK poetry magazine *Kaffeeklatsch* and is currently working on translations of the poetry of Ma Yan and other Chinese younger poets.

STEVE RIEP（饶博荣）is the professor of Chinese and comparative literature, specializing in modern and contemporary Chinese literature, film and culture. He is also co-director of International Cinema Program at Brigham Young University. A California native, he received his BA in Chinese and political economy from the University of California, Berkeley, and his PhD from the University of California, Los Angeles in modern and contemporary Chinese literature. He has translated modern and contemporary Chinese poetry, fiction, drama, and essays.